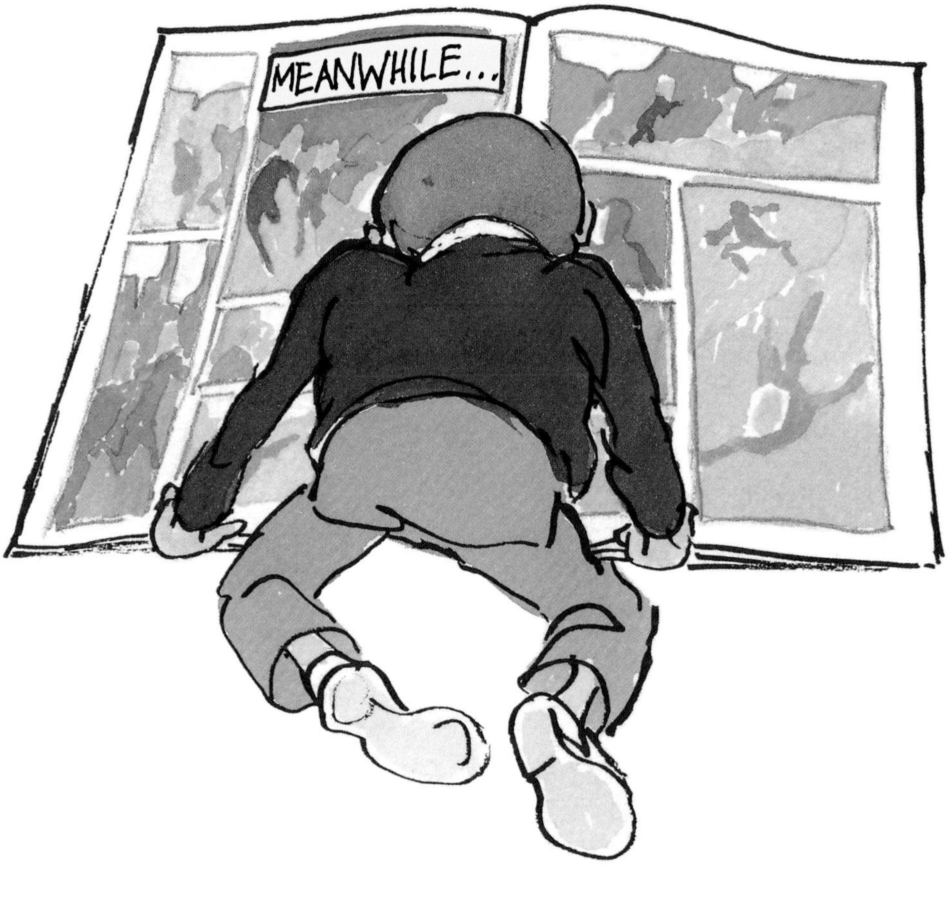
MEANWHILE...

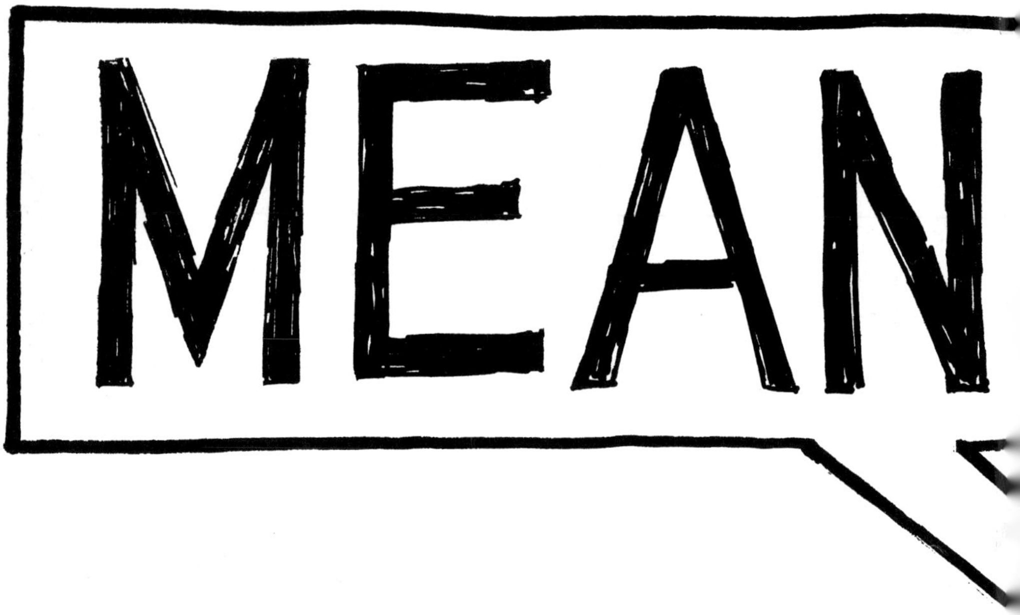
MEAN

WHILE...

...MEANWHILE

JULES FEIFFER

Michael di Capua Books ▪ HarperCollins Publishers

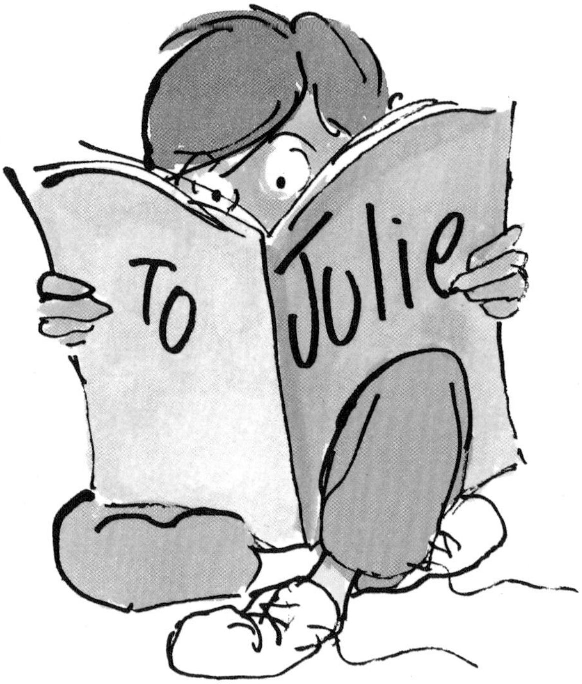
To
Julie

Library of Congress catalog card number: 97-70129
Printed in the United States of America
Designed by Steve Scott
First edition, 1997

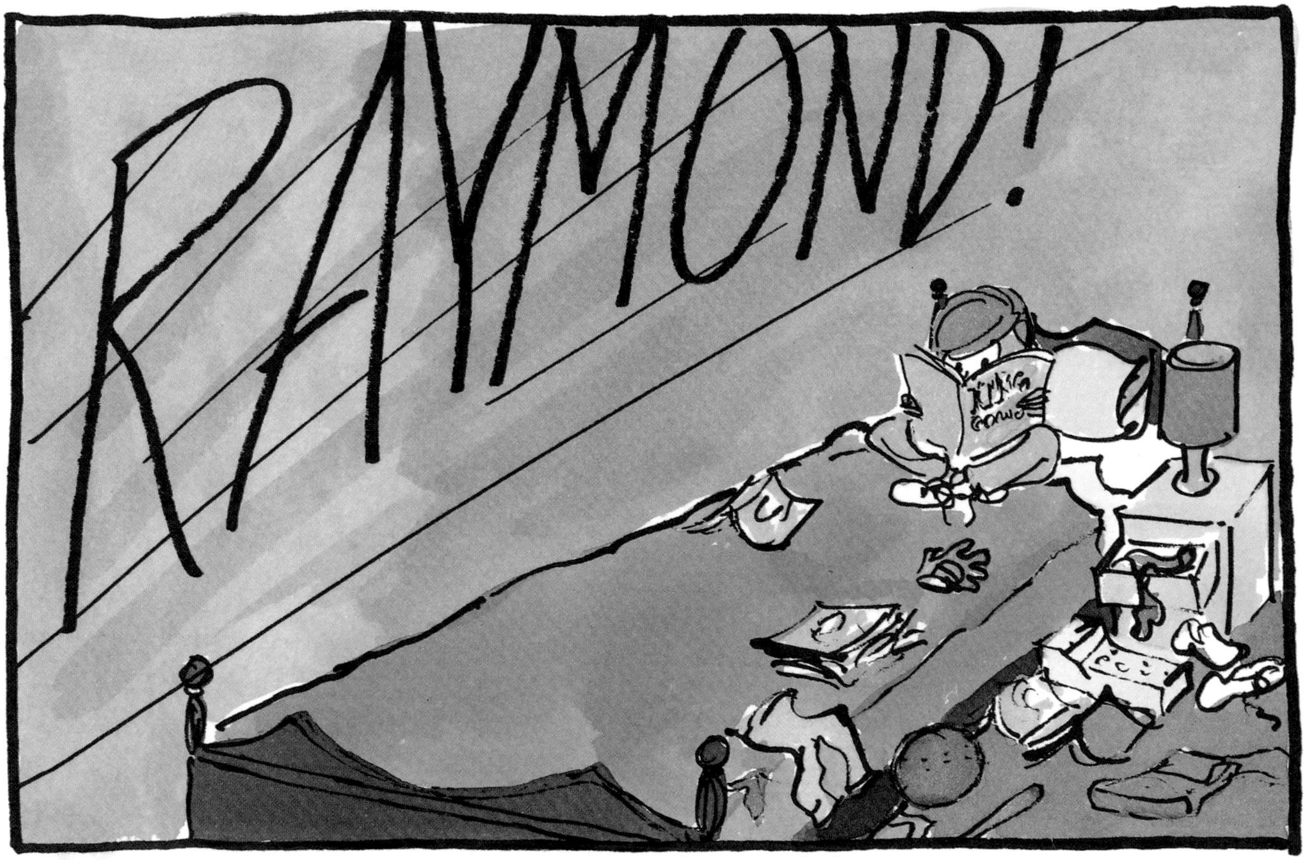
RAYMOND!

Raymond didn't hear.

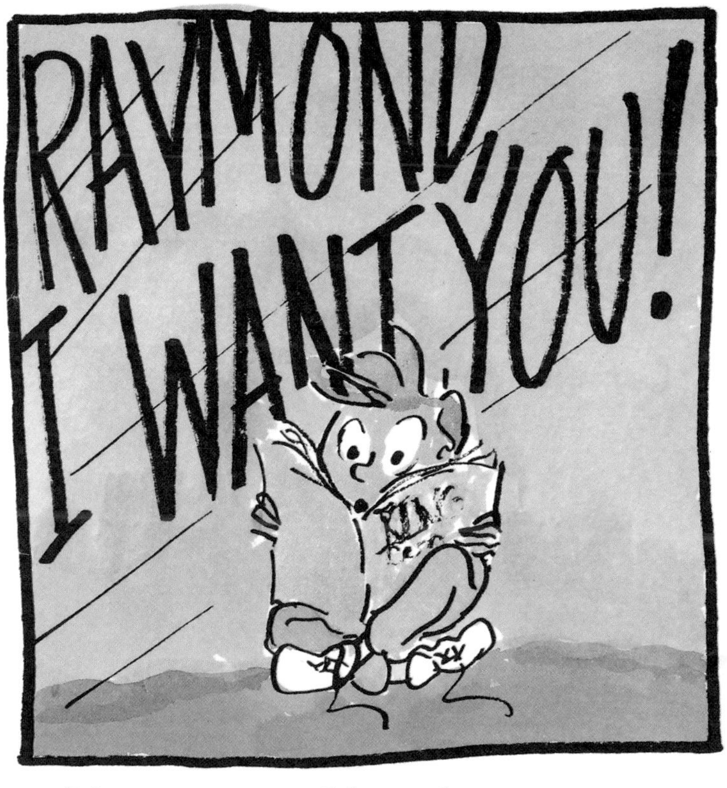
RAYMOND, I WANT YOU!

Now Raymond heard. It was his mother. She was always finding things for him to do.

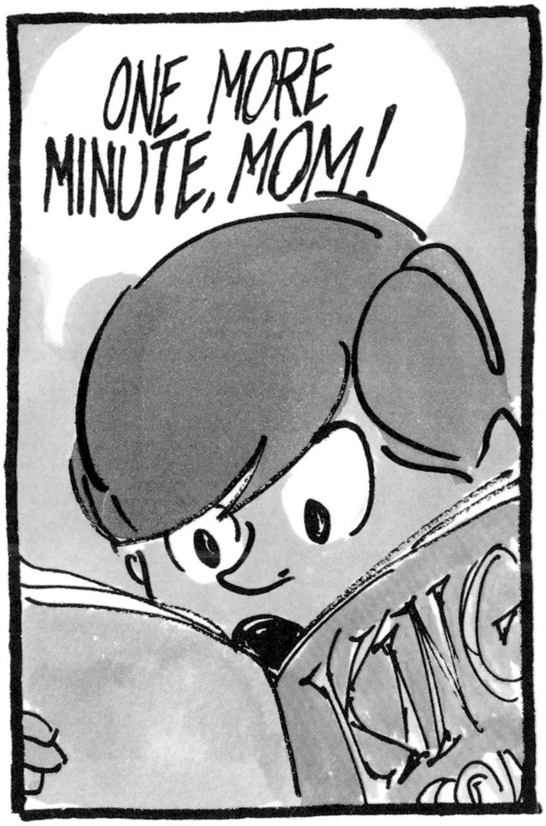
ONE MORE MINUTE, MOM!
KING

"Maybe she'll forget," thought Raymond.

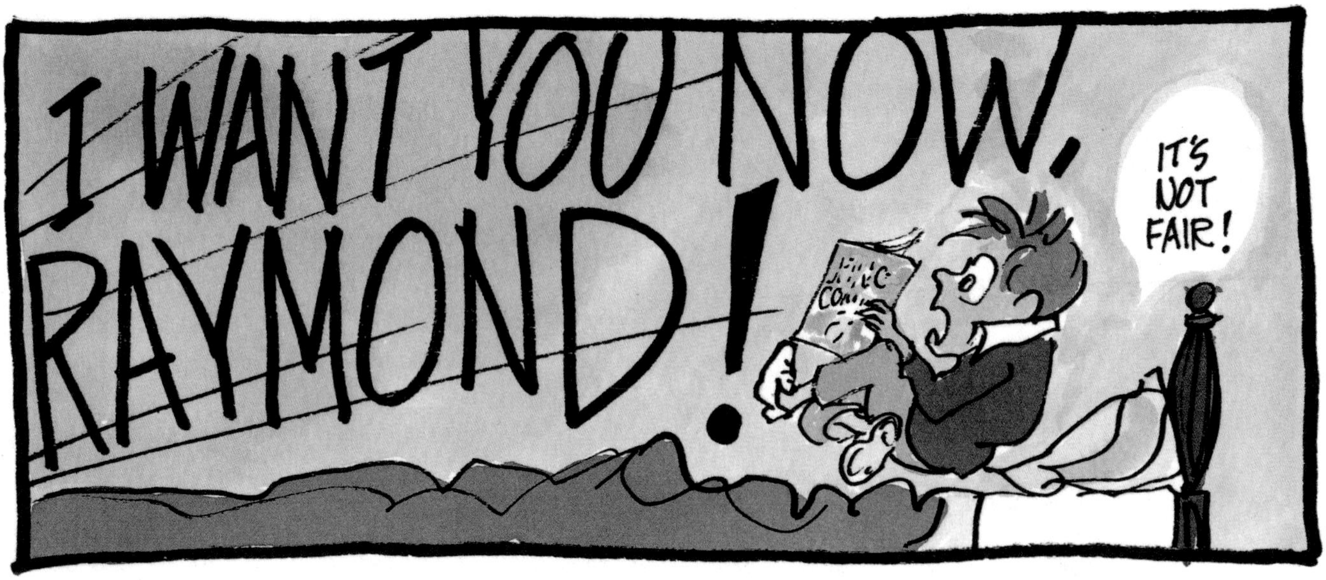
I WANT YOU NOW, RAYMOND!
IT'S NOT FAIR!

With Raymond's mother, it was always "Right now!" and never "No big deal, you can do it next Tuesday, Raymond." Suddenly . . .

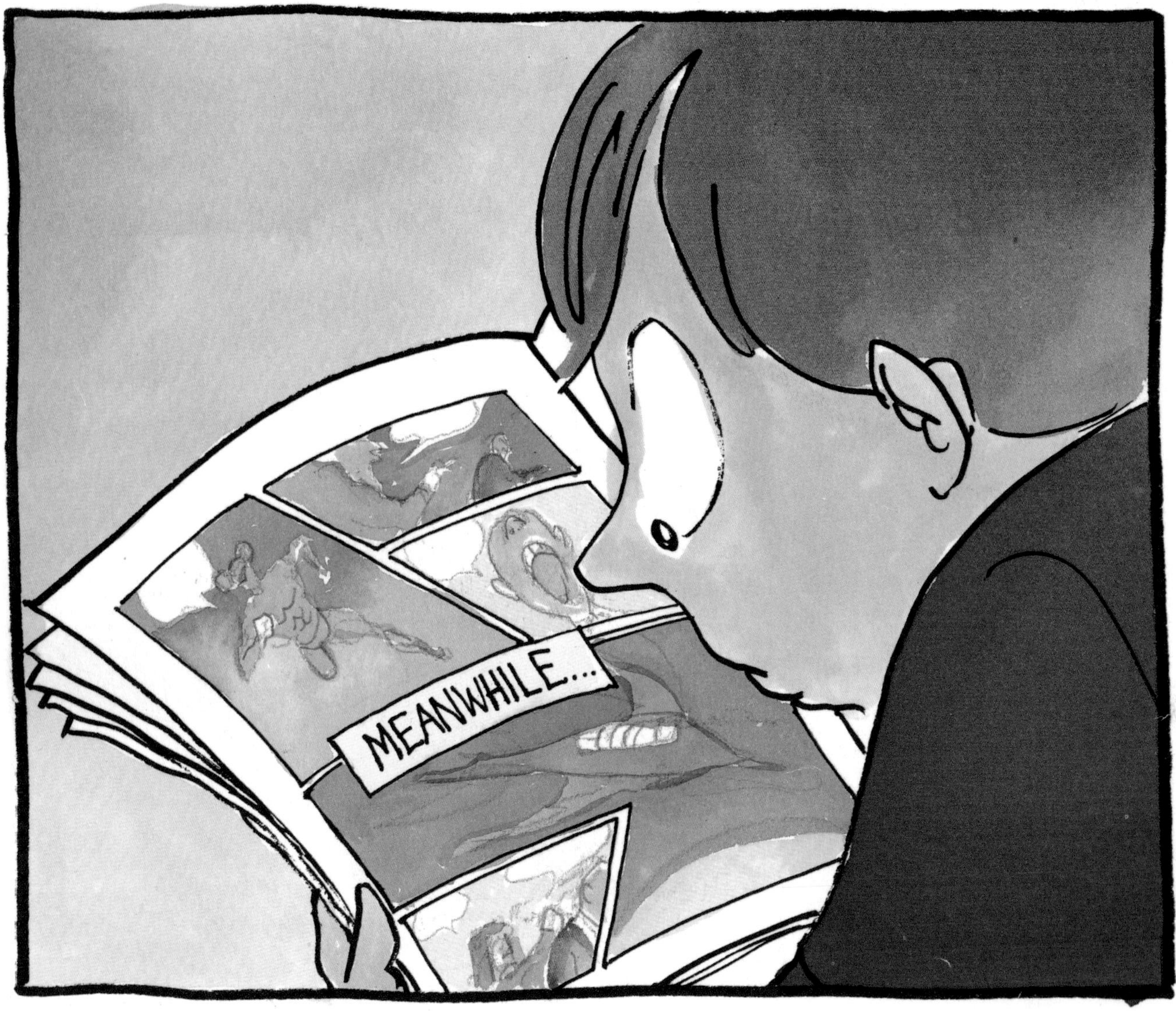
MEANWHILE...

Raymond's eye caught a word in the middle of the page.

It was a word comics always use to change the scene. MEANWHILE. But inside a box: MEANWHILE... with three dots after it. And what it meant was that wherever you were in a story, just a plain, ordinary MEANWHILE... was going to take you somewhere else.

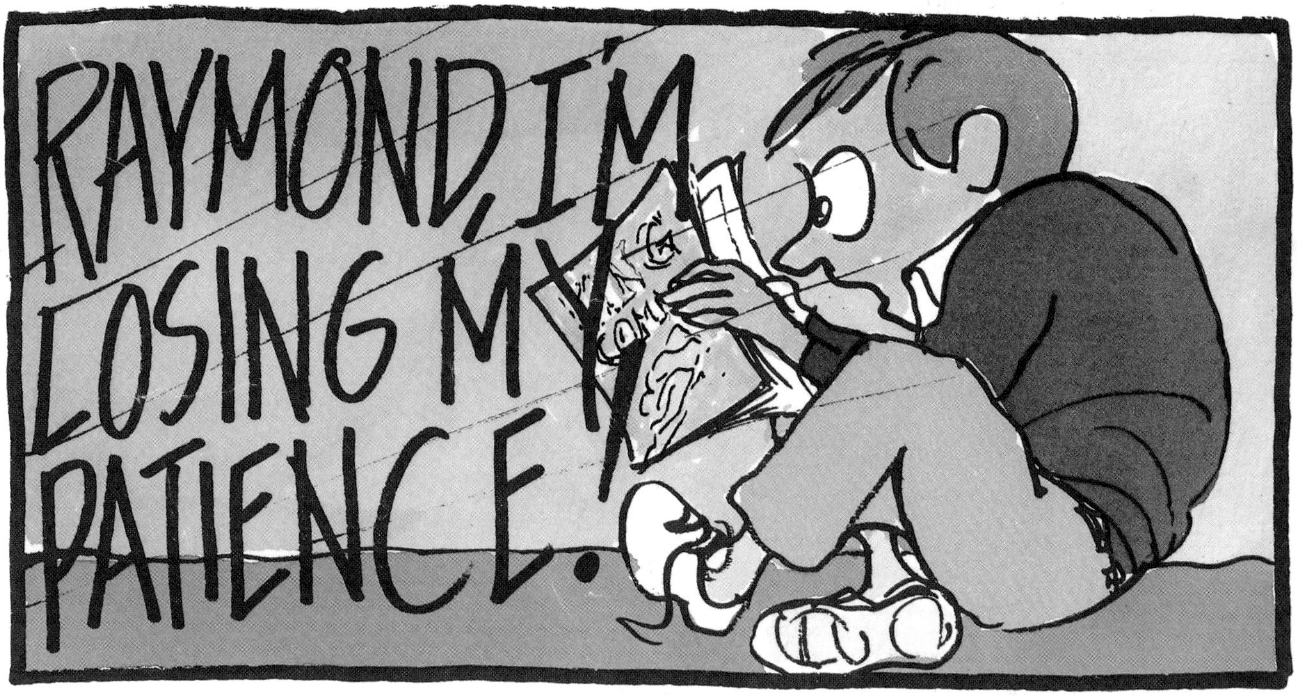
RAYMOND, I'M LOSING MY PATIENCE!

"What if I had my own MEANWHILE... ?" Raymond wondered. And with a red marker he scrawled the word on the wall behind his bed, where he hoped his mother wouldn't see it.

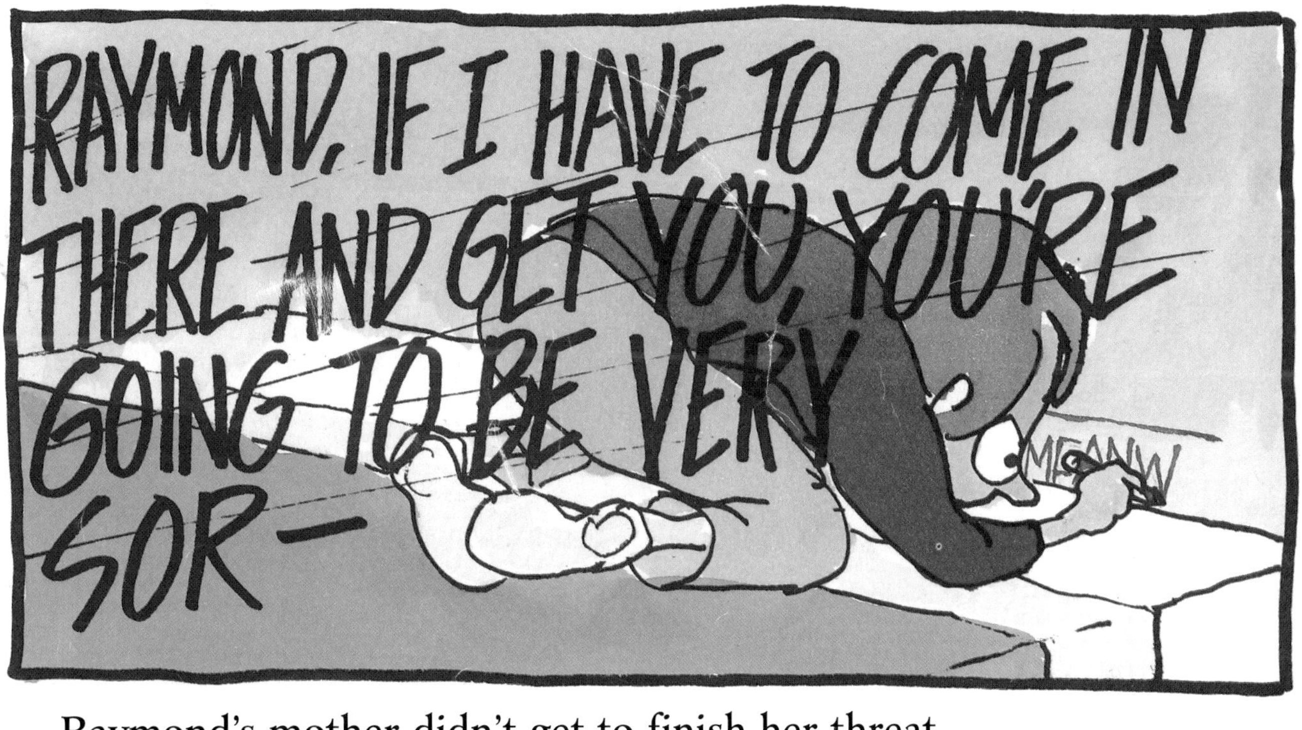
RAYMOND, IF I HAVE TO COME IN THERE AND GET YOU, YOU'RE GOING TO BE VERY SOR—
MEANW

Raymond's mother didn't get to finish her threat.

Raymond was on a pirate ship on the high seas.

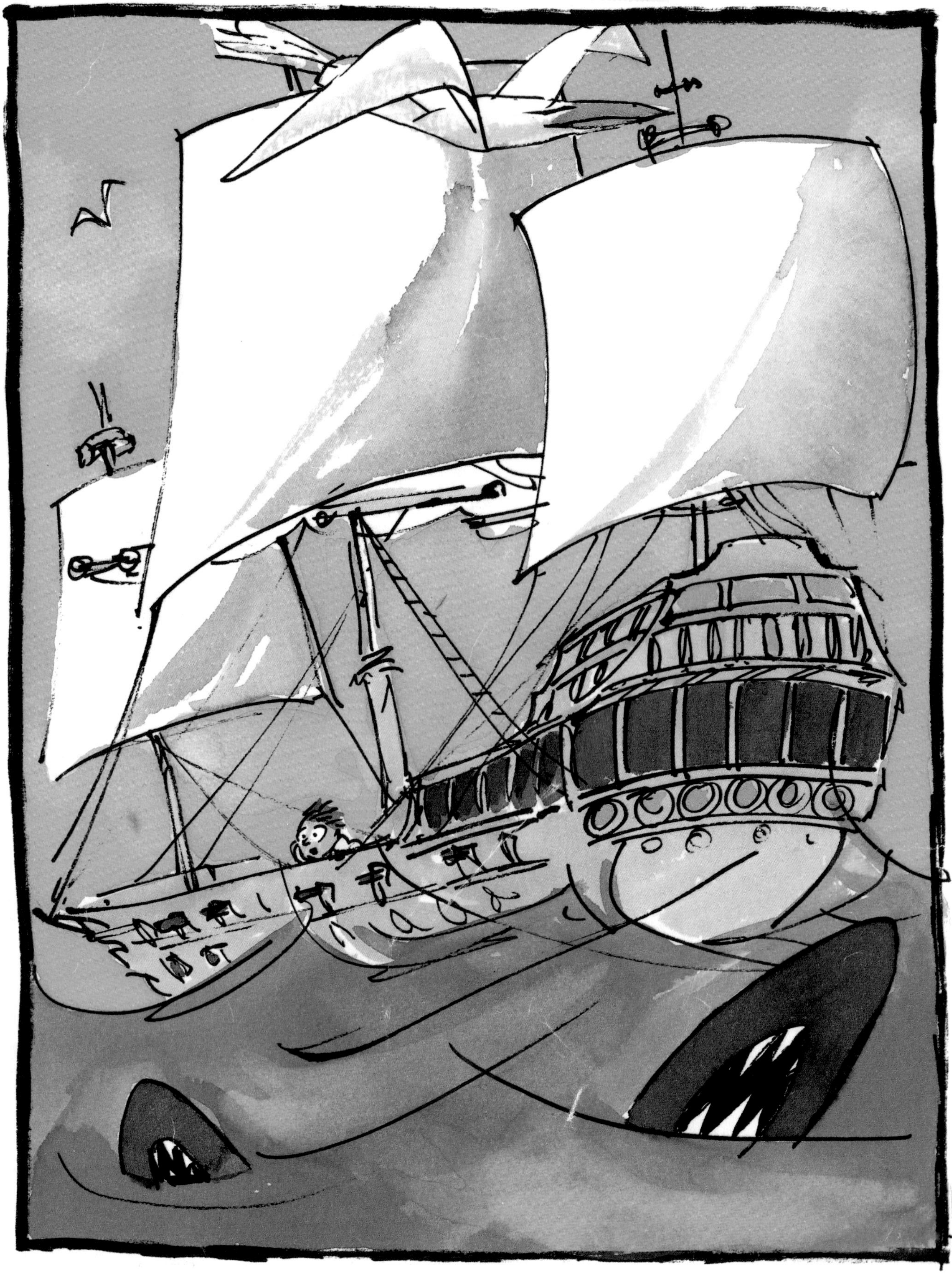

Unbelievable! He had MEANWHILED. . . !

Wicked pirates were boarding a Royal naval vessel. They were dueling the Queen's loyal sailors.

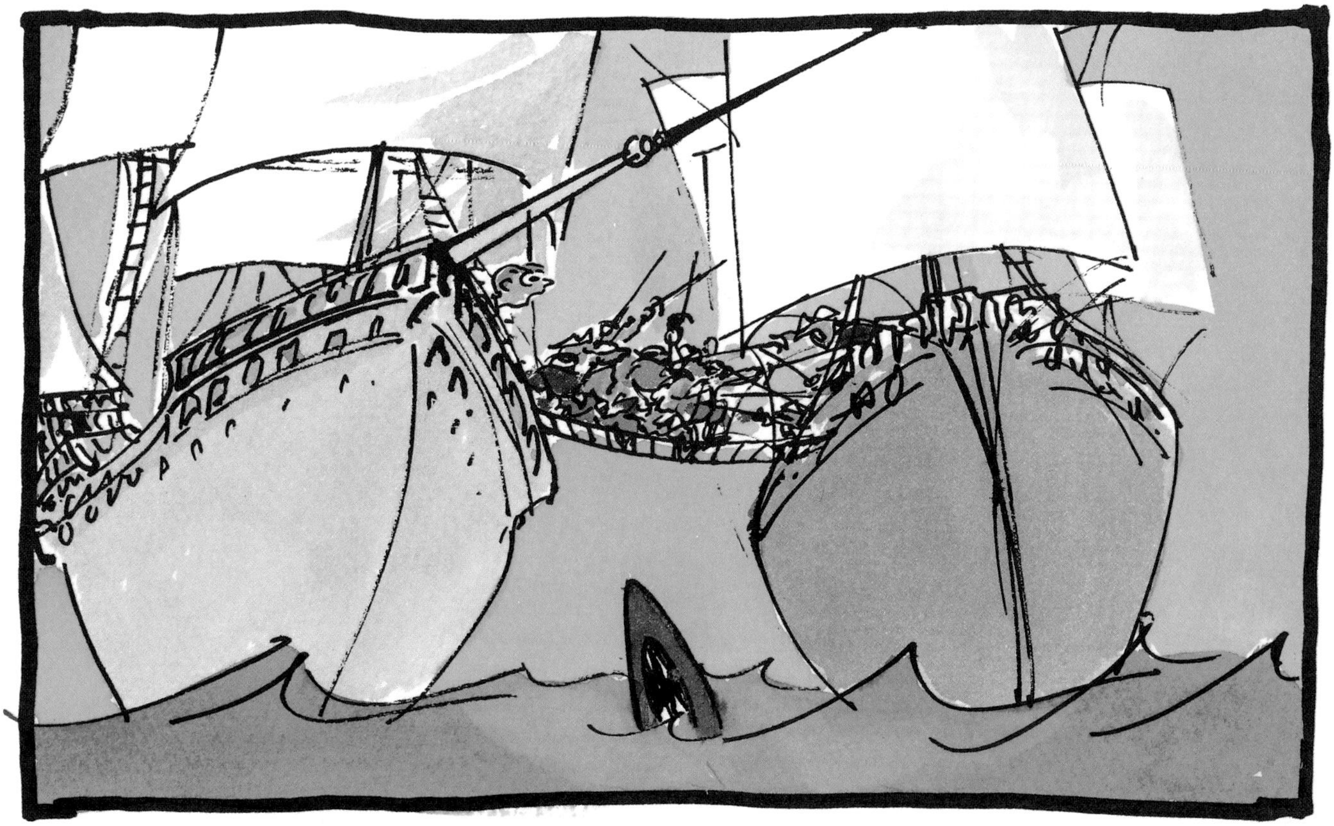

Raymond couldn't just stand by and watch as if it were a picture in a comic book.

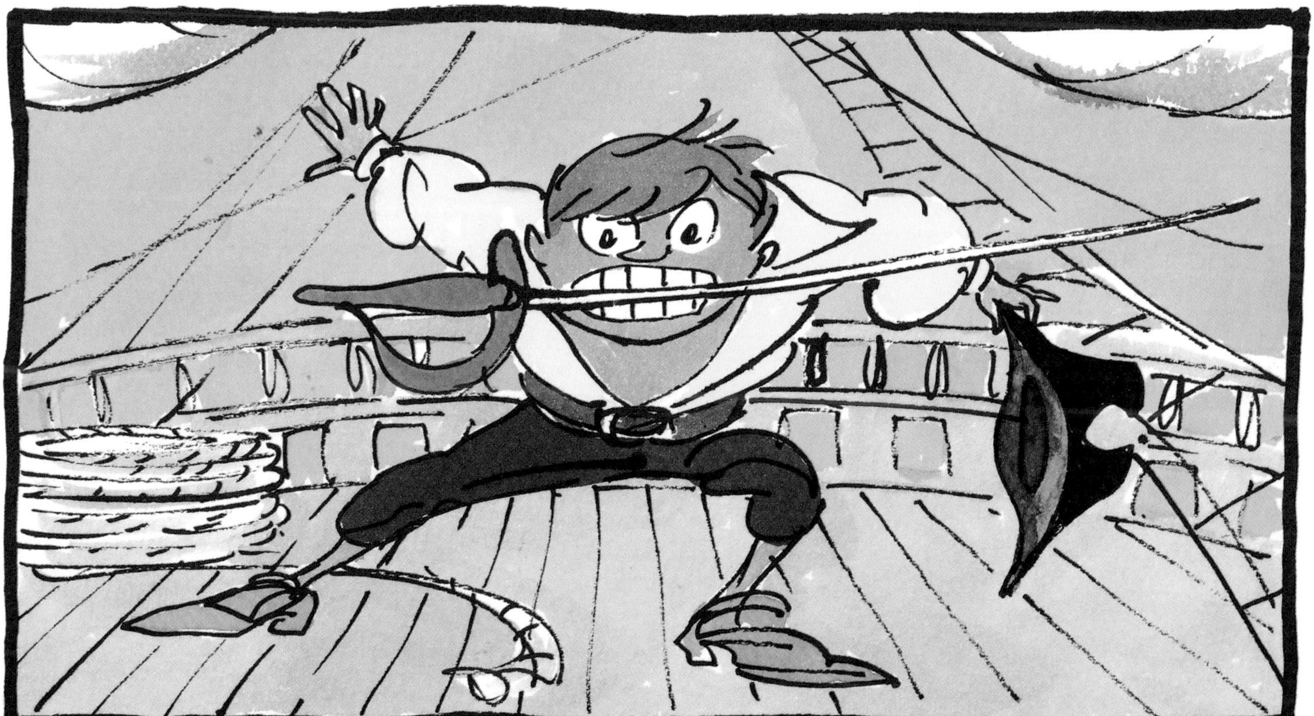

He clenched a sword between his teeth . . .

Then swung by a rope over the shark-infested sea onto the Royal naval vessel.

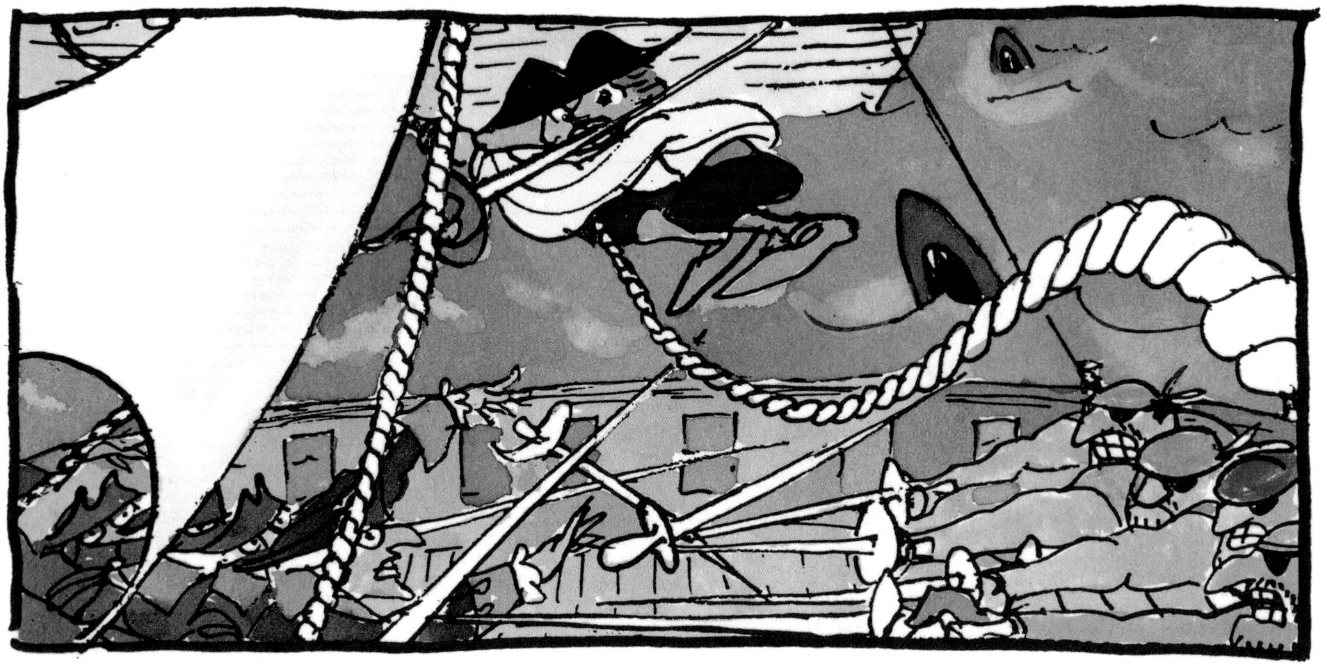

He dueled the wicked pirates singlehanded. And also rescued a beautiful maiden.

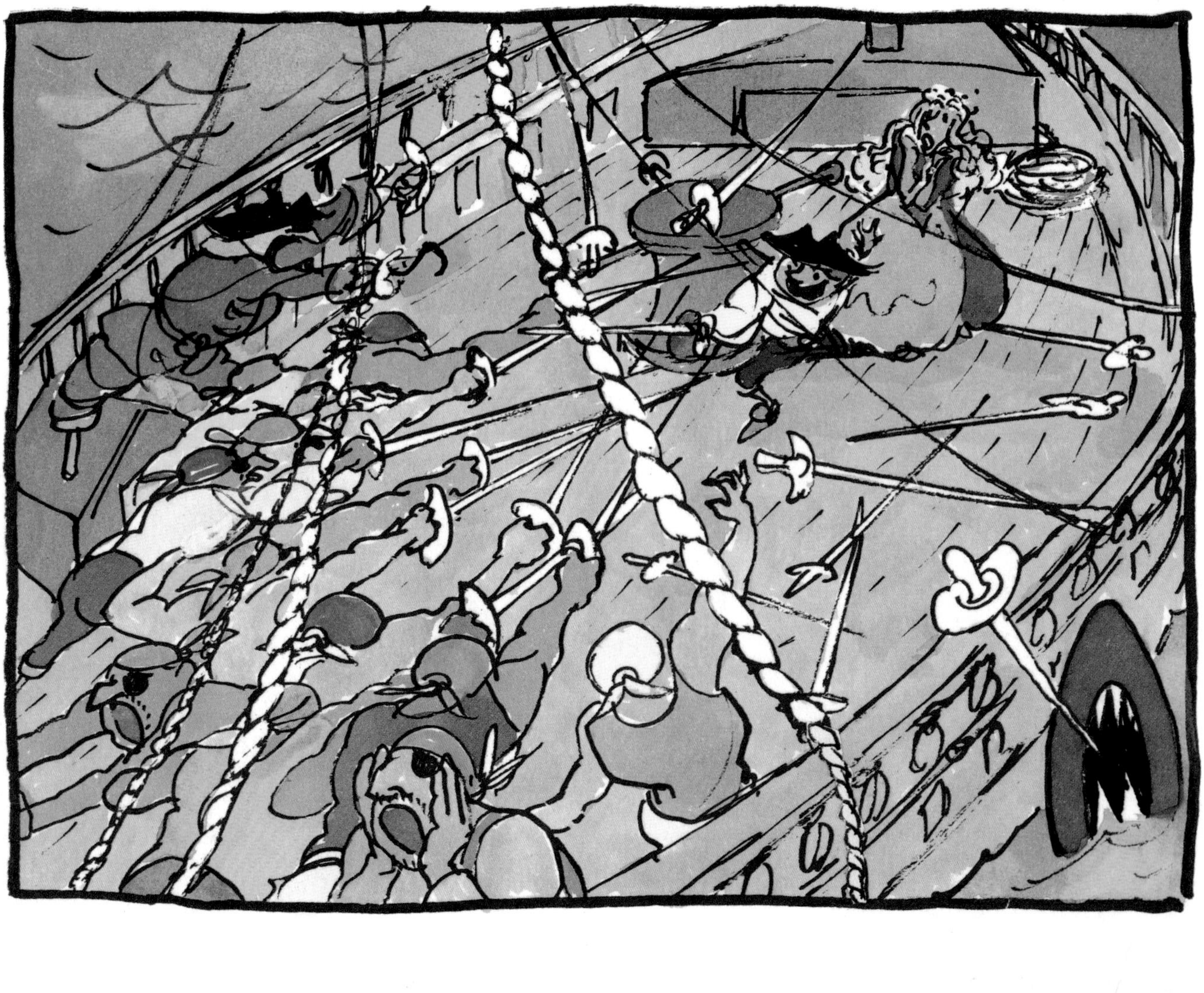

The only reason he didn't capture the pirate captain was his sword broke.

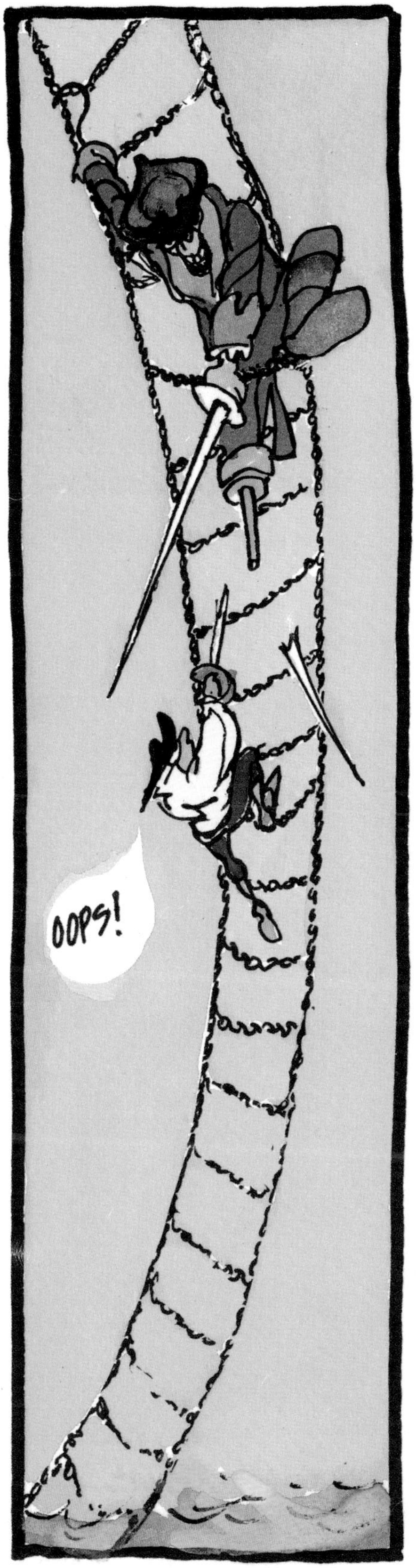
OOPS!

So Raymond was forced to walk the plank. The situation was hopeless.

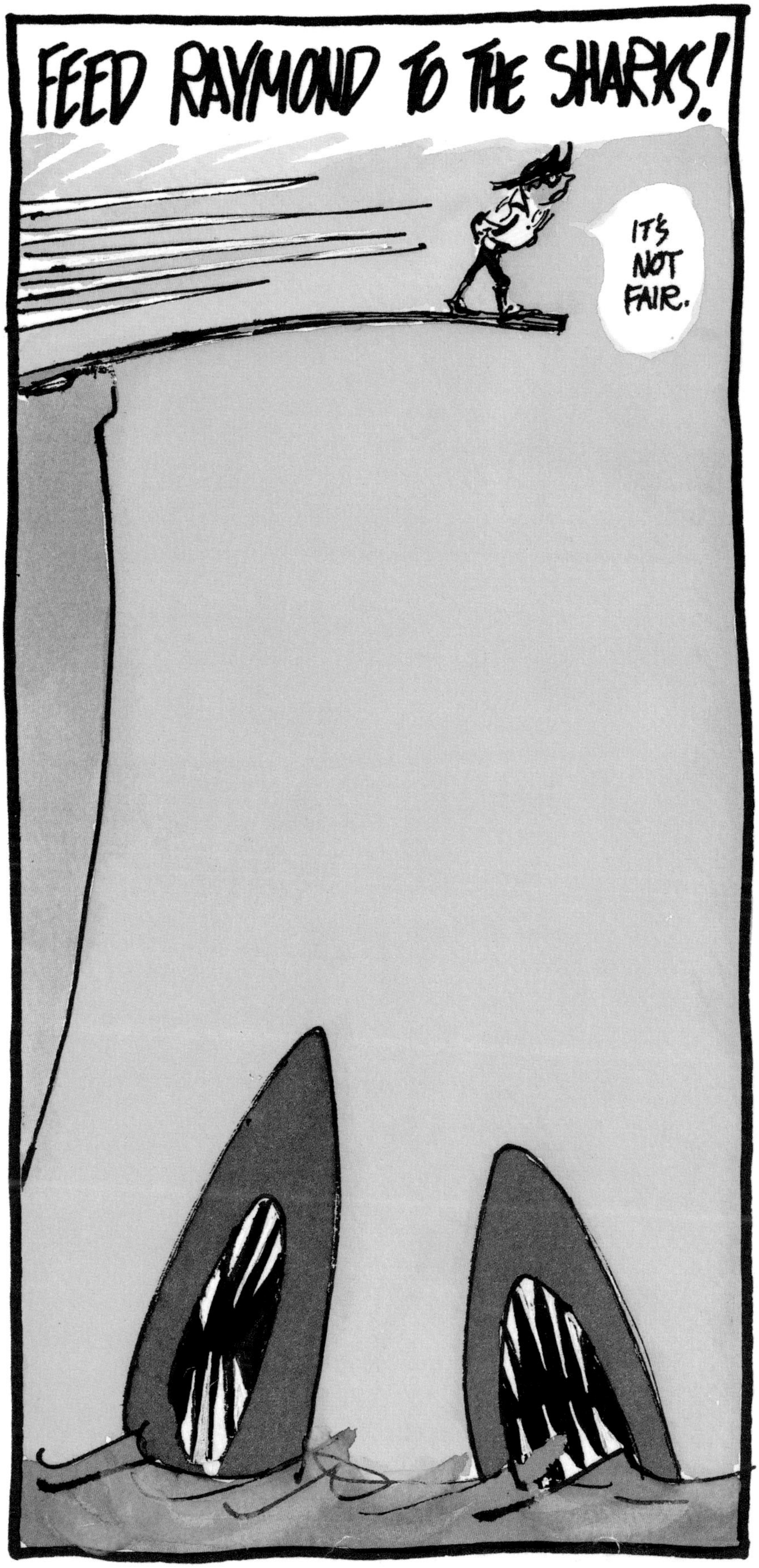
FEED RAYMOND TO THE SHARKS!
IT'S NOT FAIR.

Raymond knew he had one last chance to save himself.

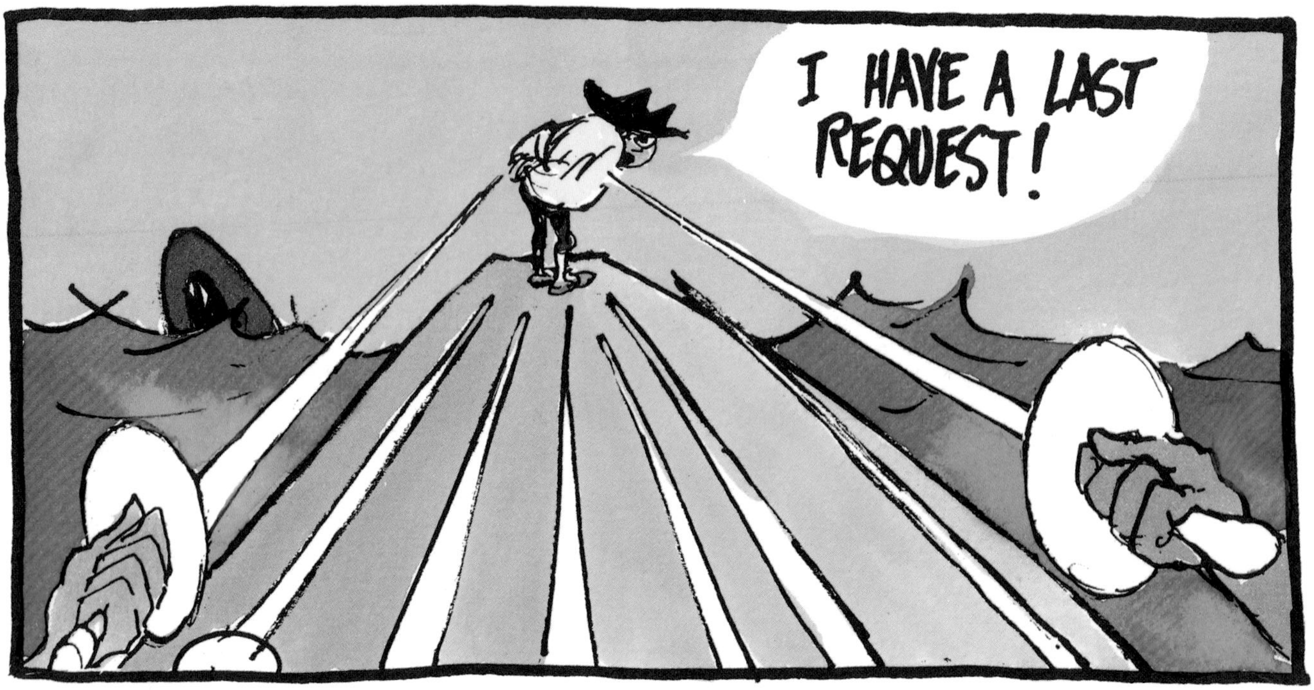
I HAVE A LAST REQUEST!

"It's the law of the sea that I have to grant you your last request," grumbled the Captain, who had a hook and a peg leg and a patch on one eye. And so did the rest of his crew.

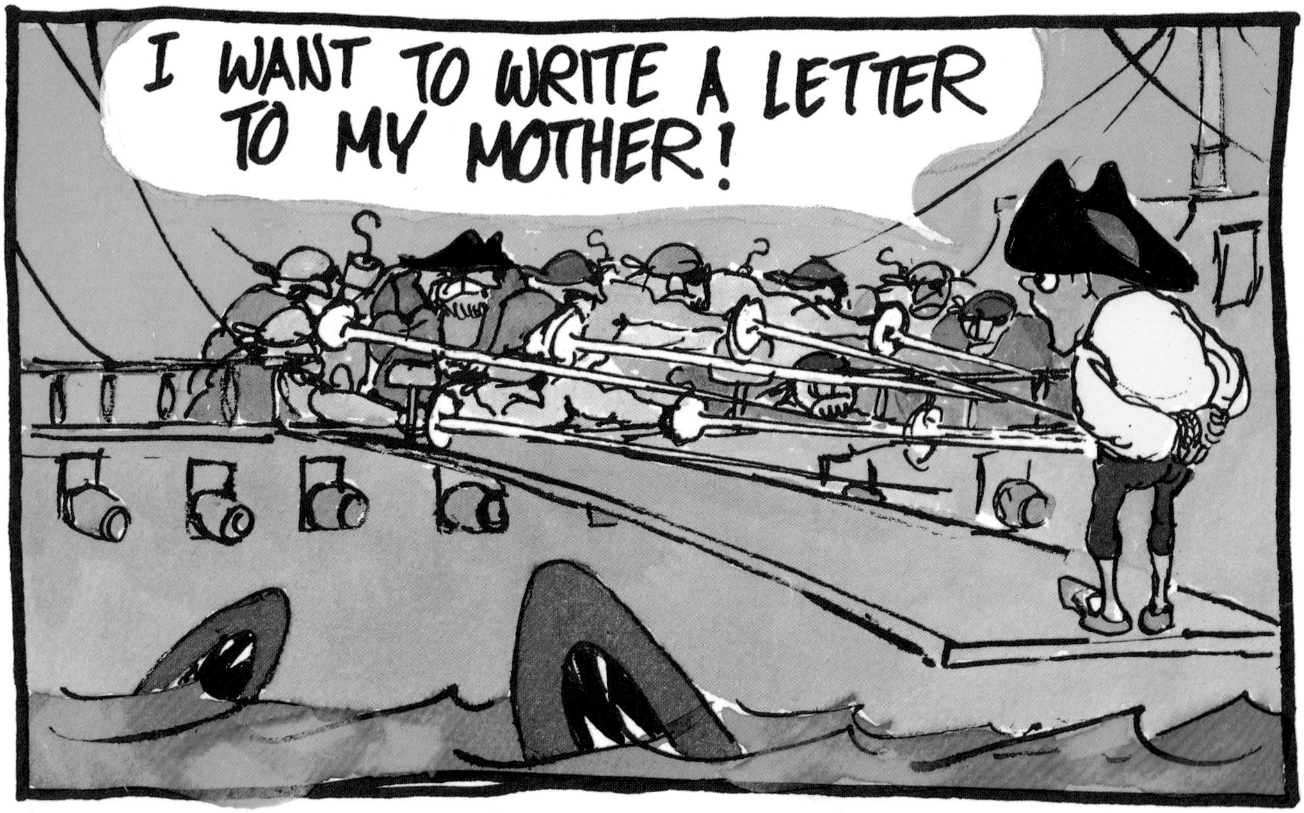
I WANT TO WRITE A LETTER TO MY MOTHER!

But none of the pirates had anything to write with. And why should they? None of them could read.

"Wait!" cried the beautiful maiden.

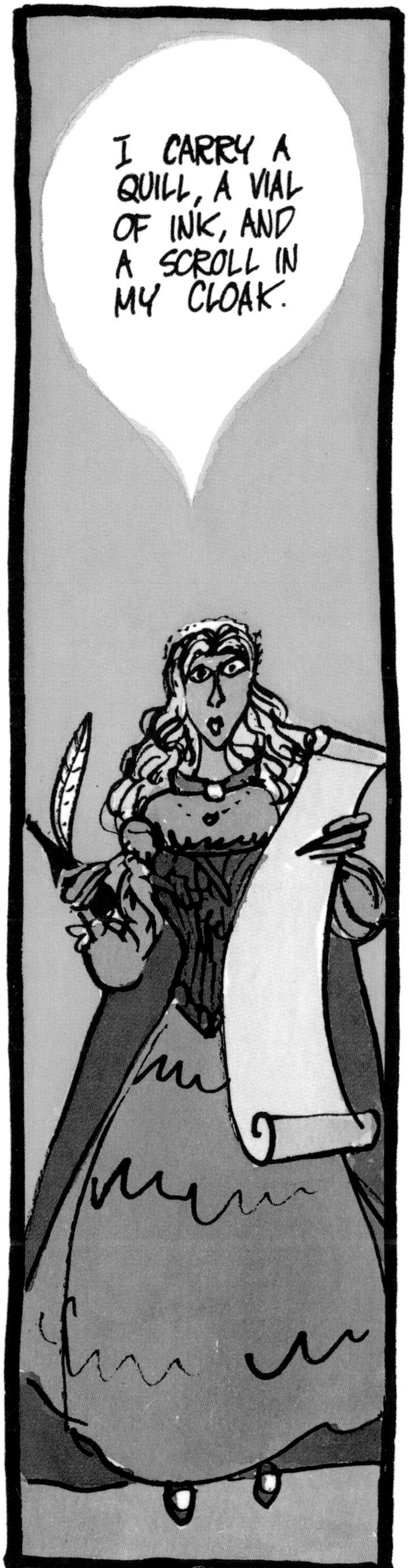
I CARRY A QUILL, A VIAL OF INK, AND A SCROLL IN MY CLOAK.

So right there on the plank, Raymond wrote on the scroll: MEANWHILE…

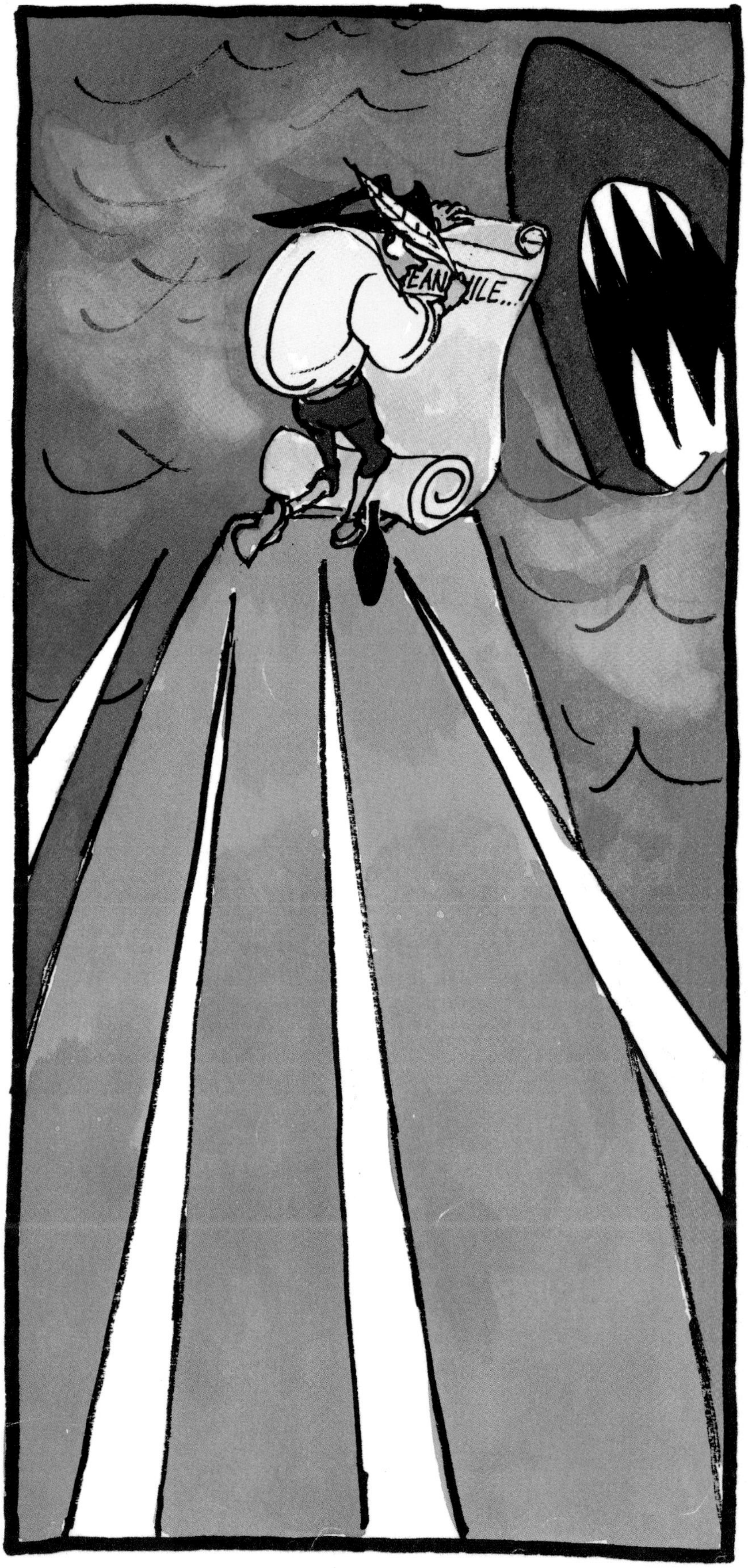
MEANWHILE...

Raymond was out West, being chased by a posse.

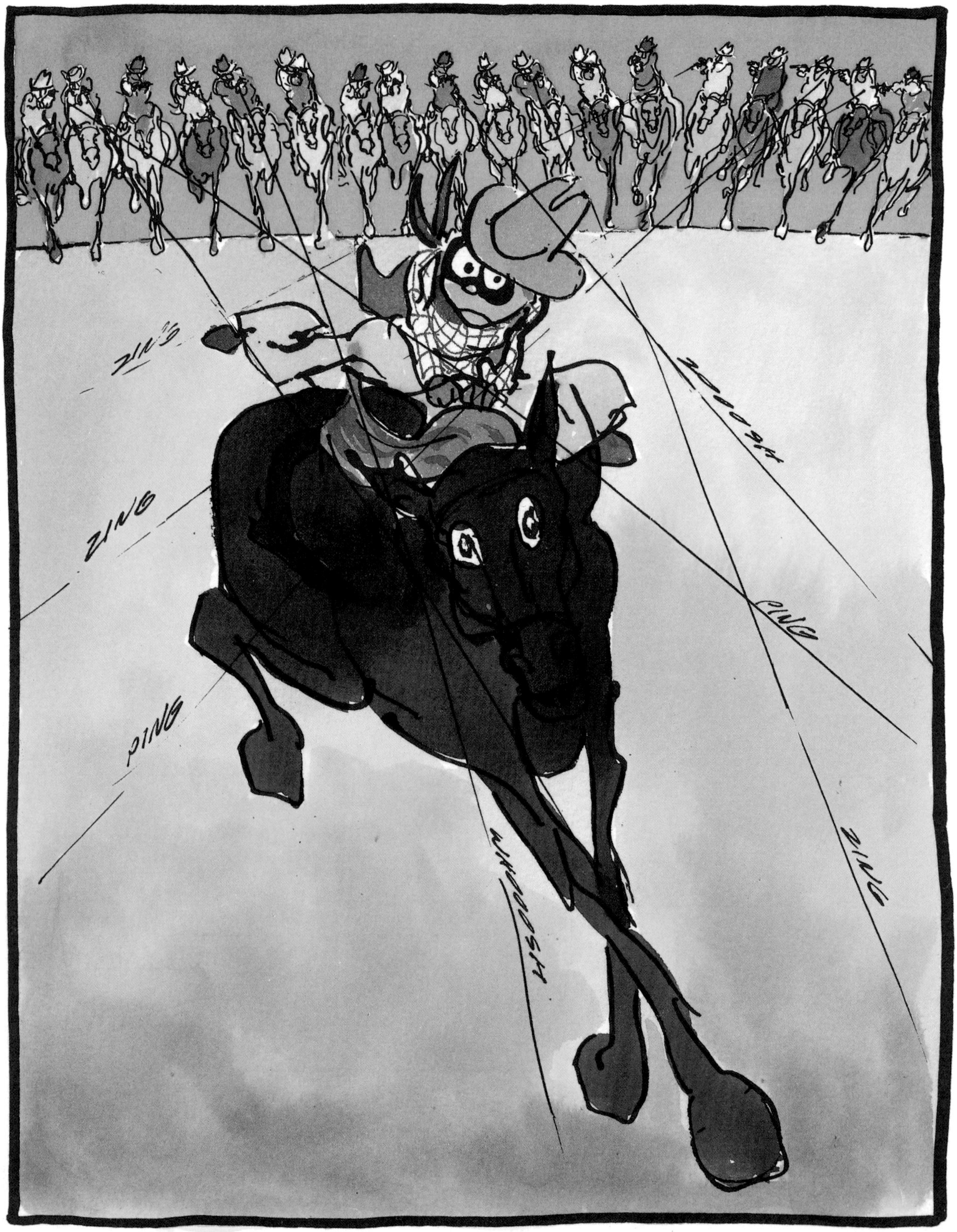
ZING
ZING
PING
PING
ZING

He didn't know why. Maybe because he was wearing a mask and they mistook him for an outlaw.

Raymond tried to reason with the posse.

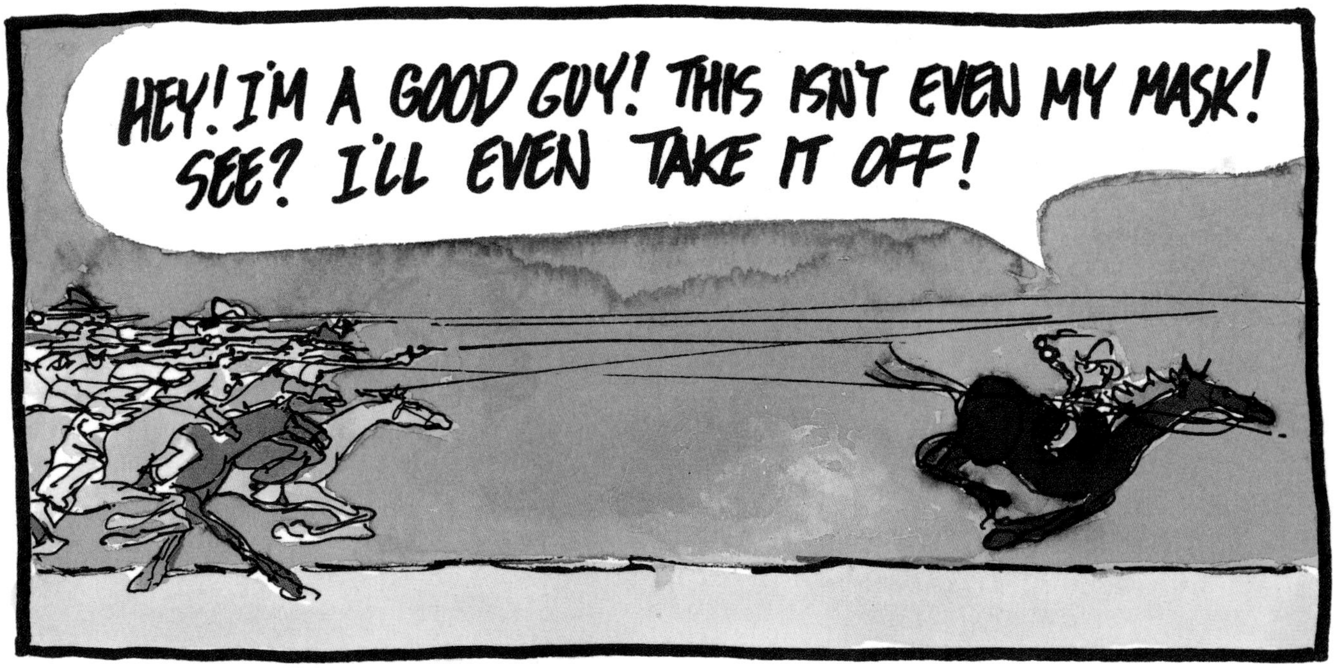
HEY! I'M A GOOD GUY! THIS ISN'T EVEN MY MASK! SEE? I'LL EVEN TAKE IT OFF!

But the posse couldn't care less. They kept shooting.

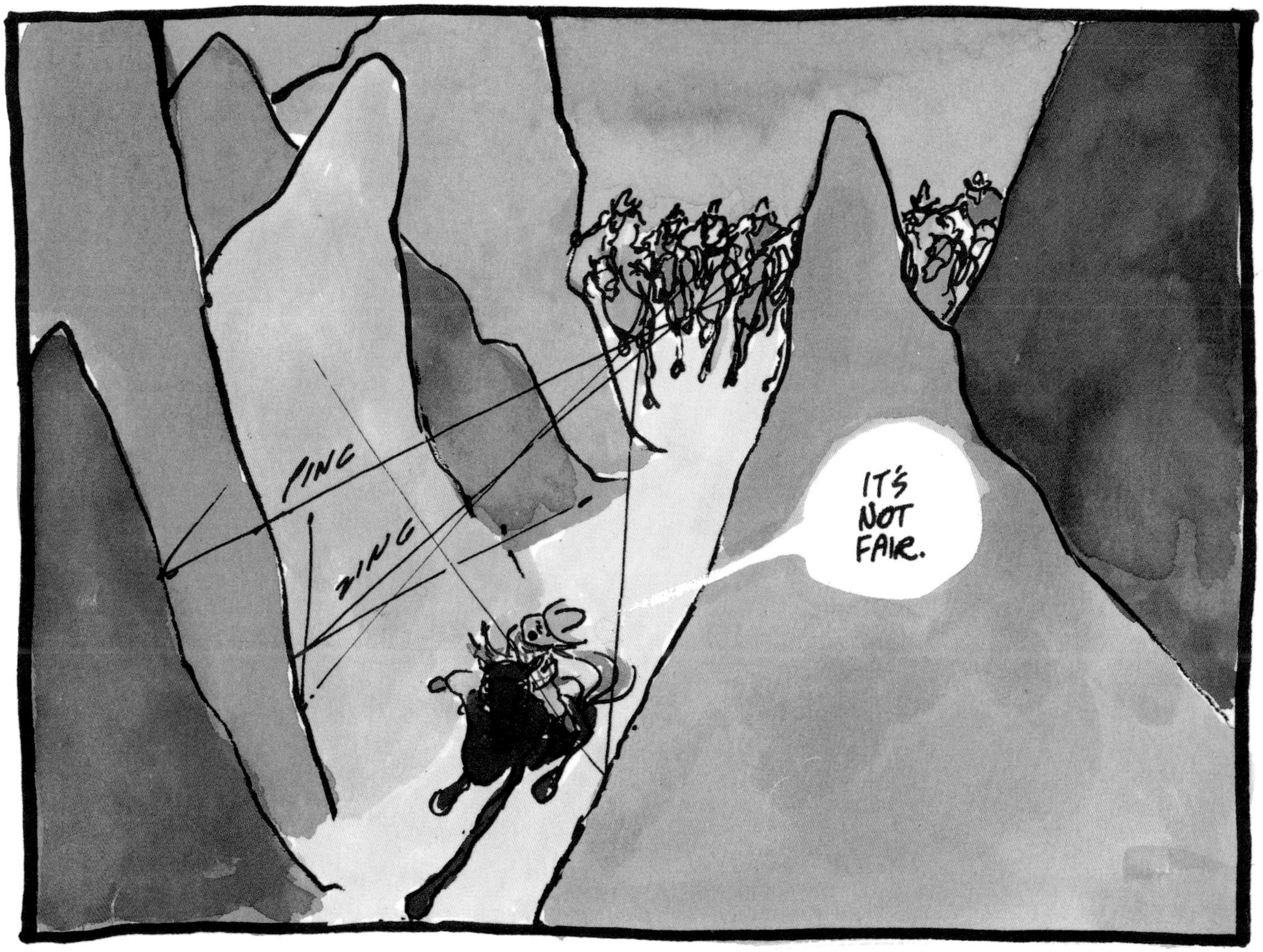
PING
ZING
IT'S NOT FAIR.

Raymond made a sharp left and galloped into a canyon . . .

Right into an avalanche!

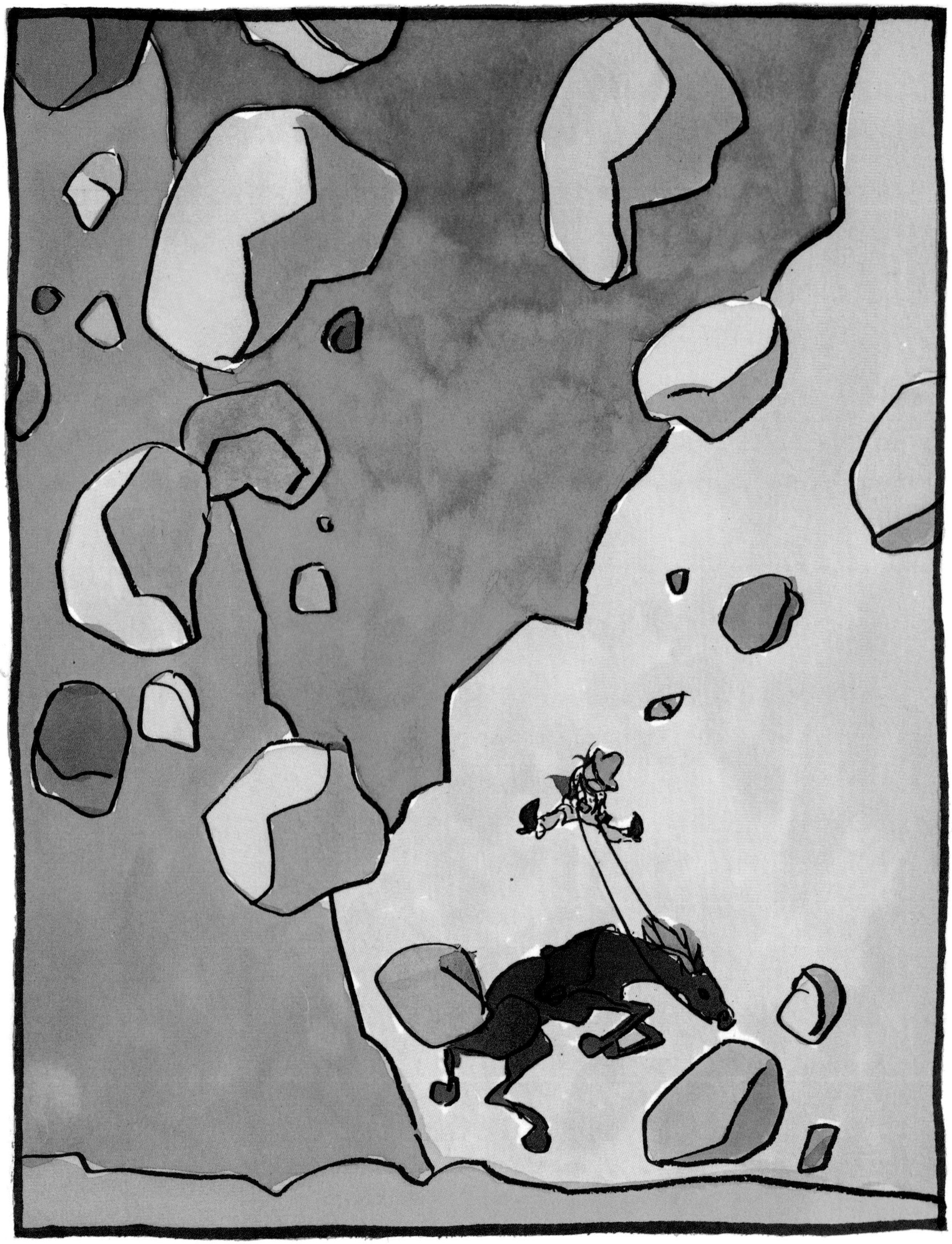

Lucky for Raymond, he was a great trick rider. He maneuvered his horse to miss the falling rocks.

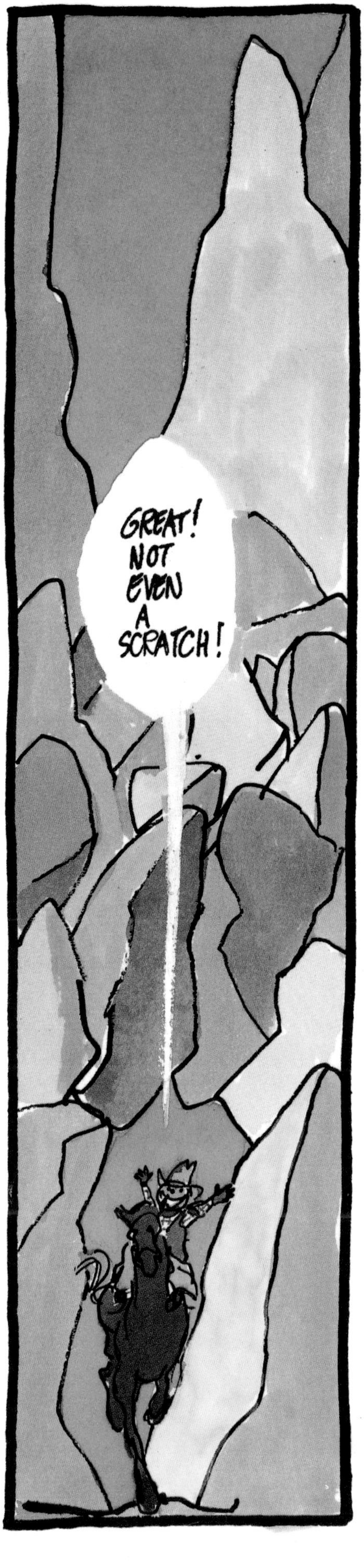
GREAT! NOT EVEN A SCRATCH!

Raymond did not see the ferocious mountain lion . . .

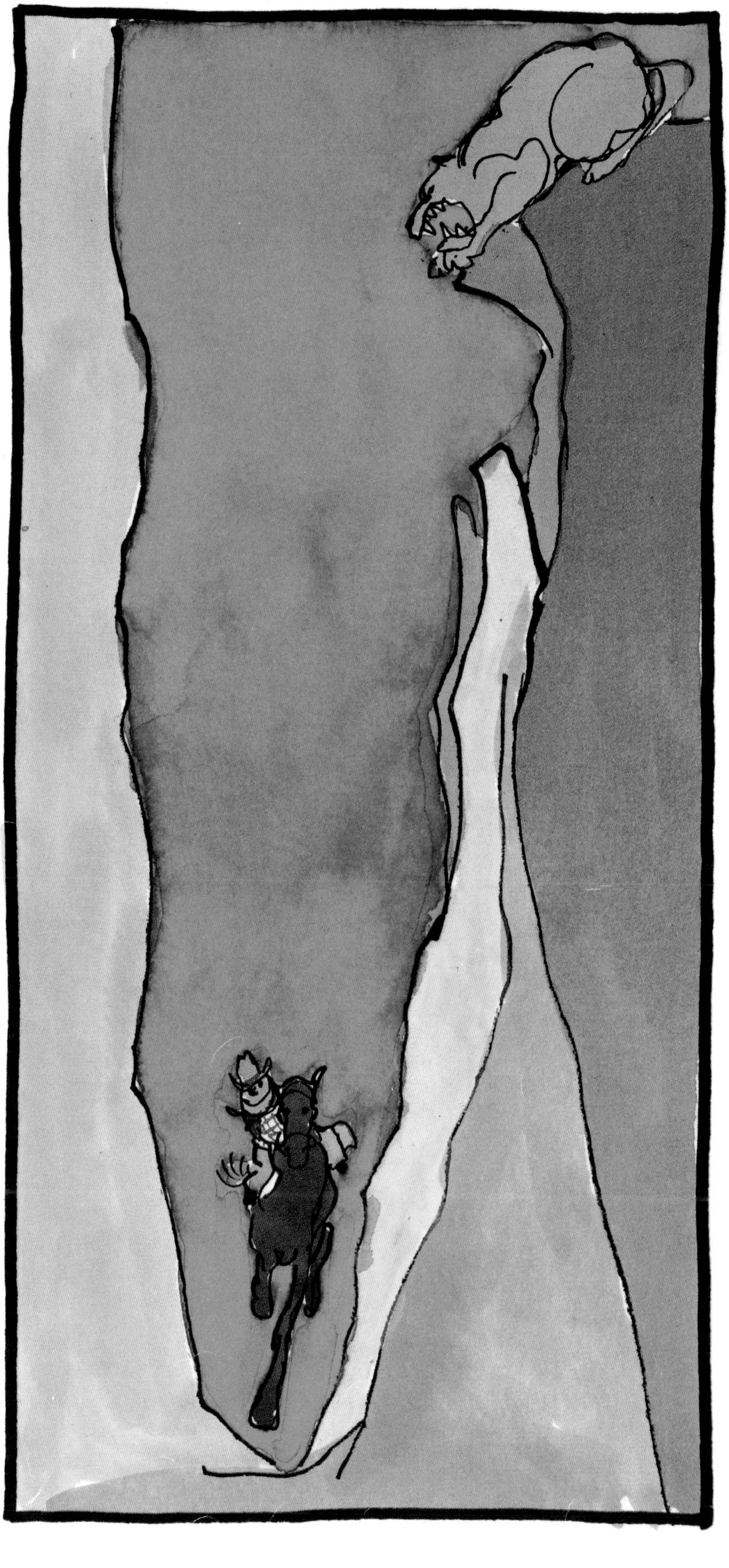

Until it was almost too late. He reached for his gun.

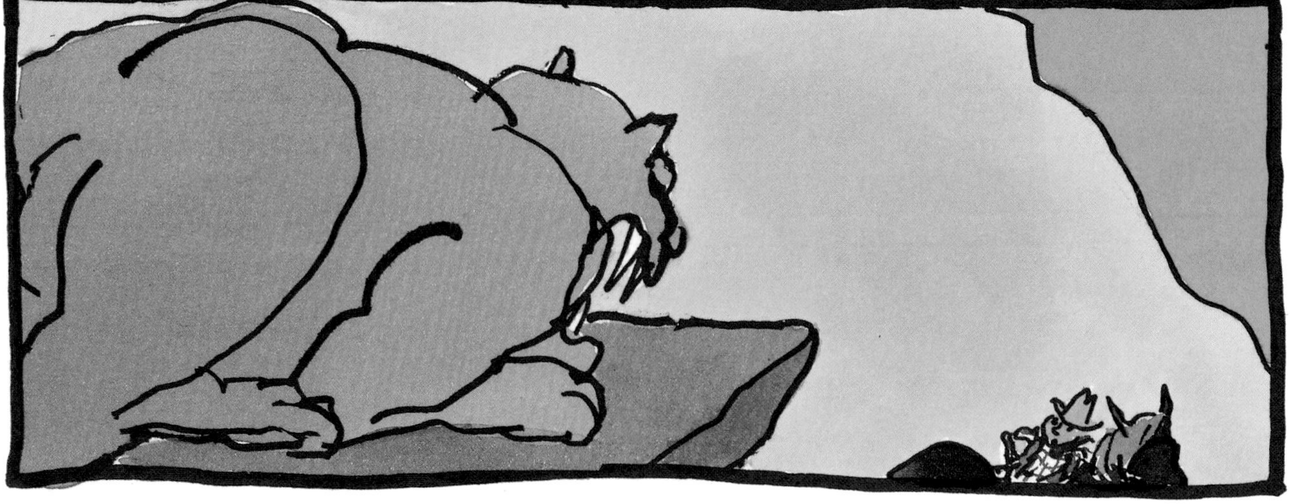

He didn't have a gun.

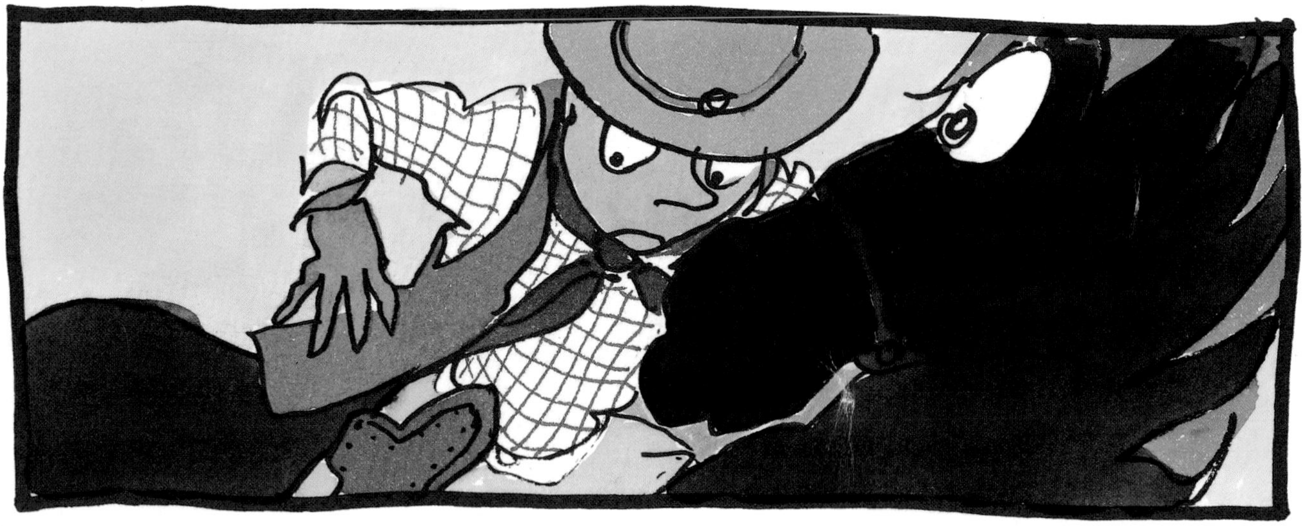

How could he be a cowboy out West and not have a gun?

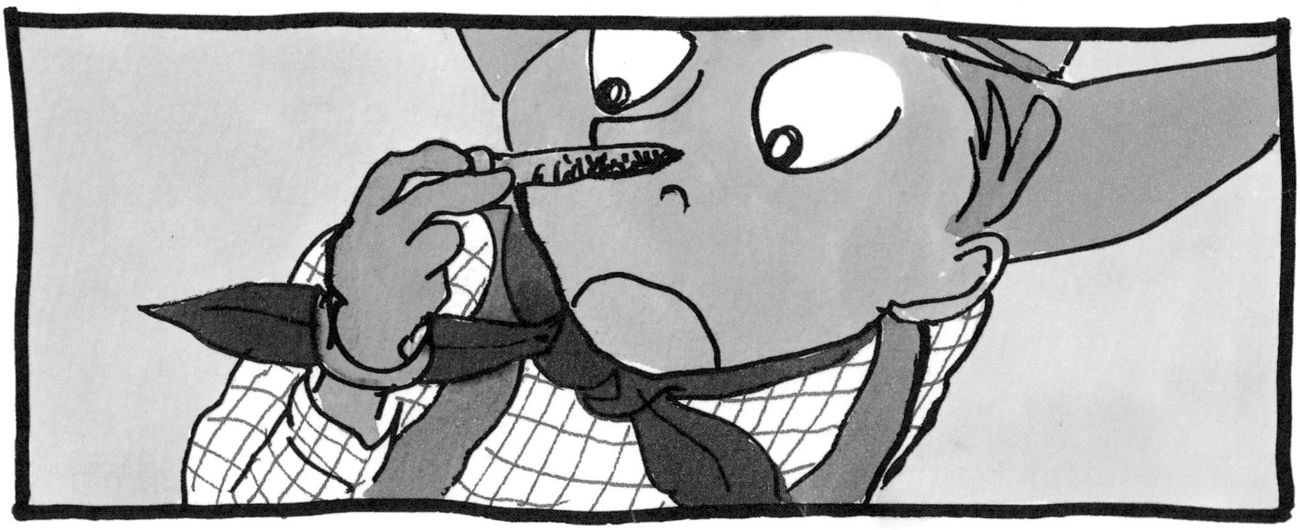

The only thing he found in his holster was a rusty bullet.

The mountain lion leaped. The situation was hopeless.

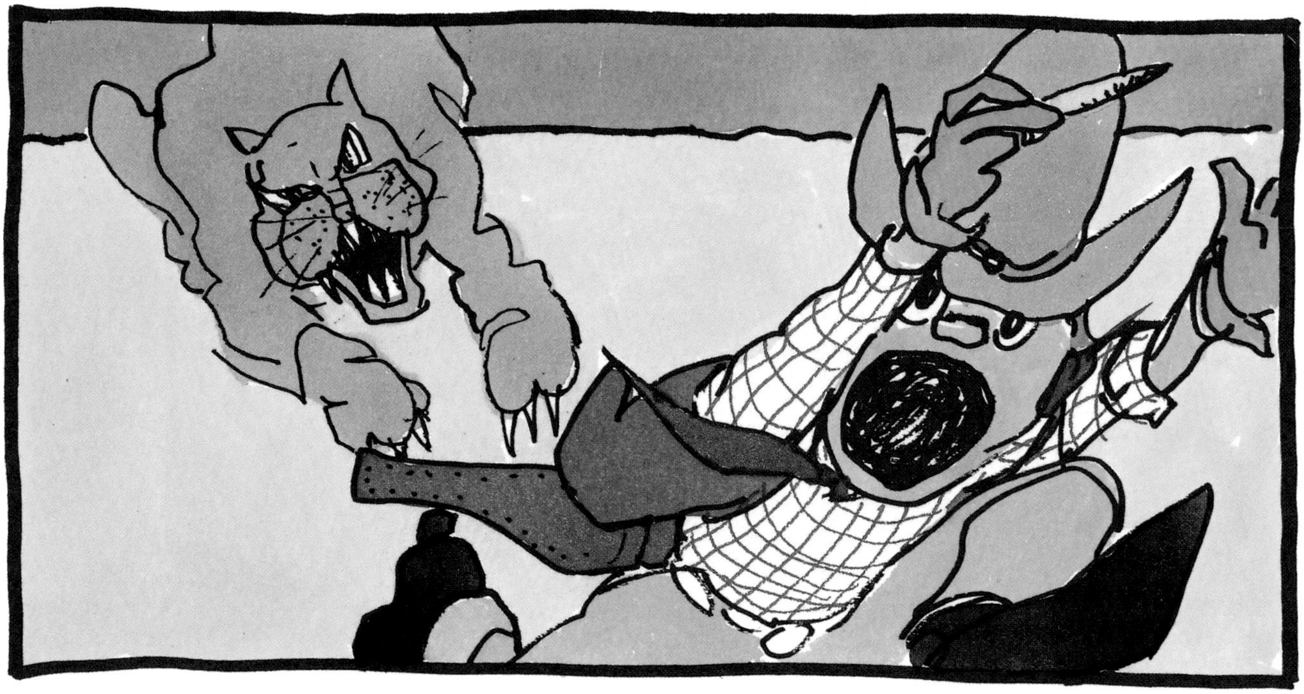

Raymond knew he had one last chance to save himself. He made a mad dash over to the nearest rock, and with the pointy end of the rusty bullet he scratched out: MEANWHILE...

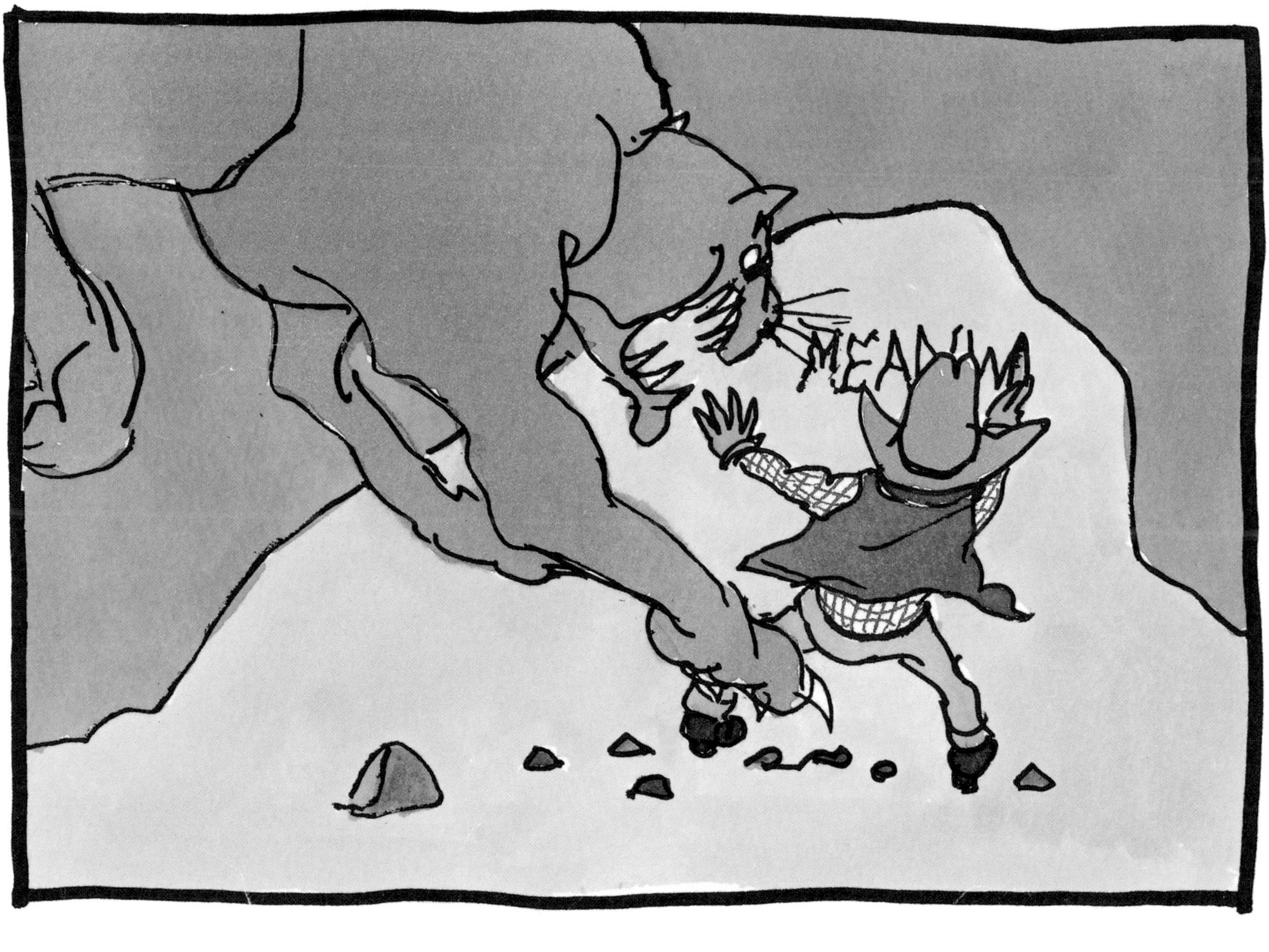

Raymond was in outer space, being chased by Martians.

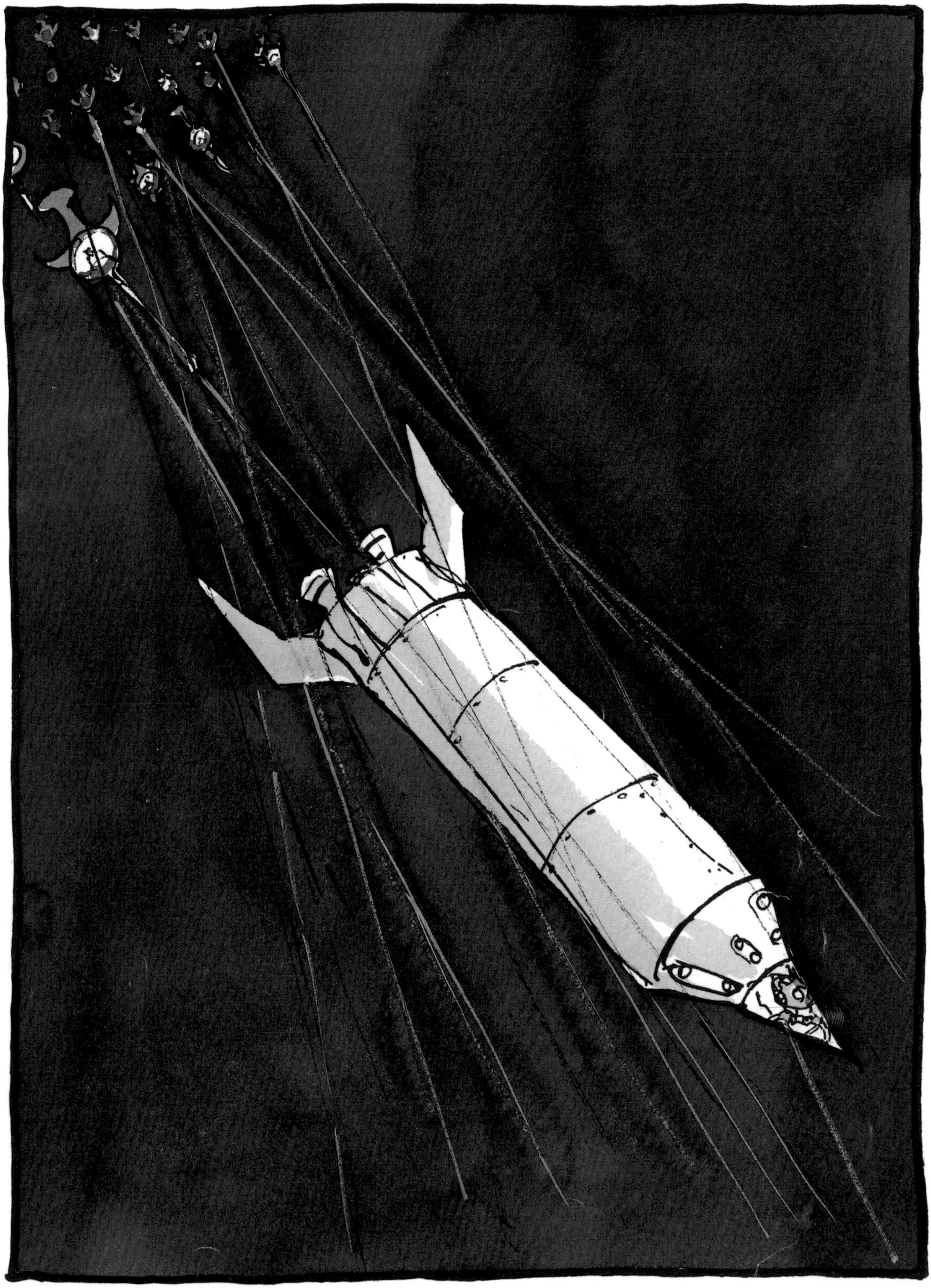

He evened the odds against him by shooting down 112 Martian spaceships.

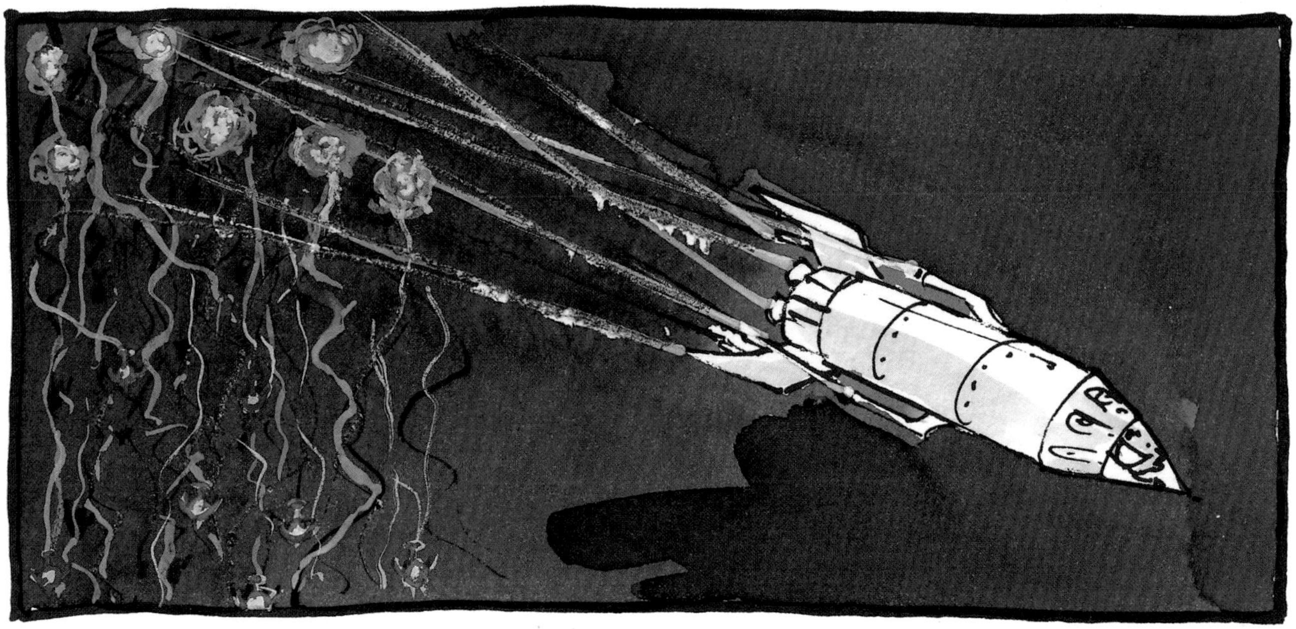

The evil two-headed King of the Martians got in a lucky shot.

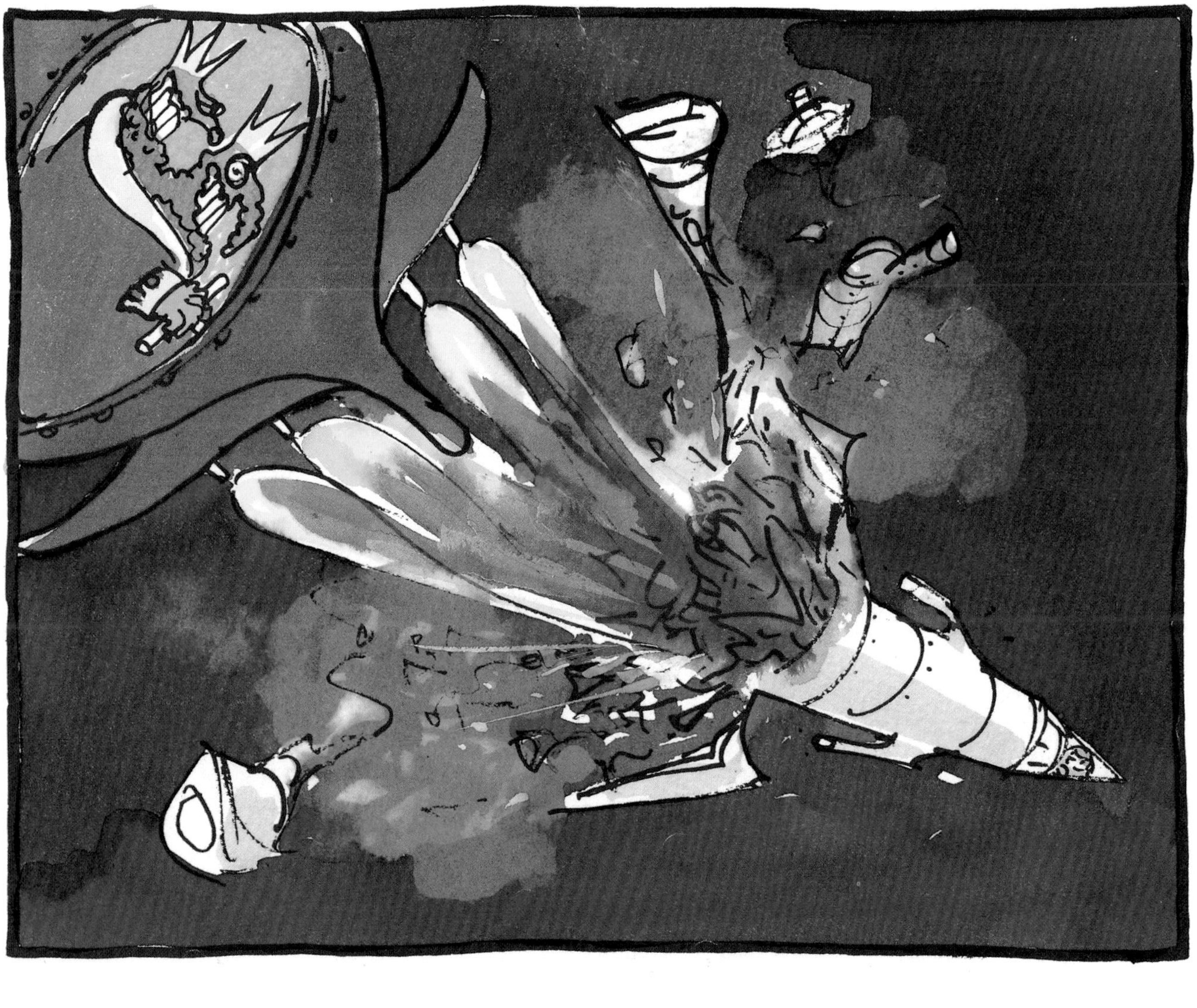

Raymond lost his aft . . .

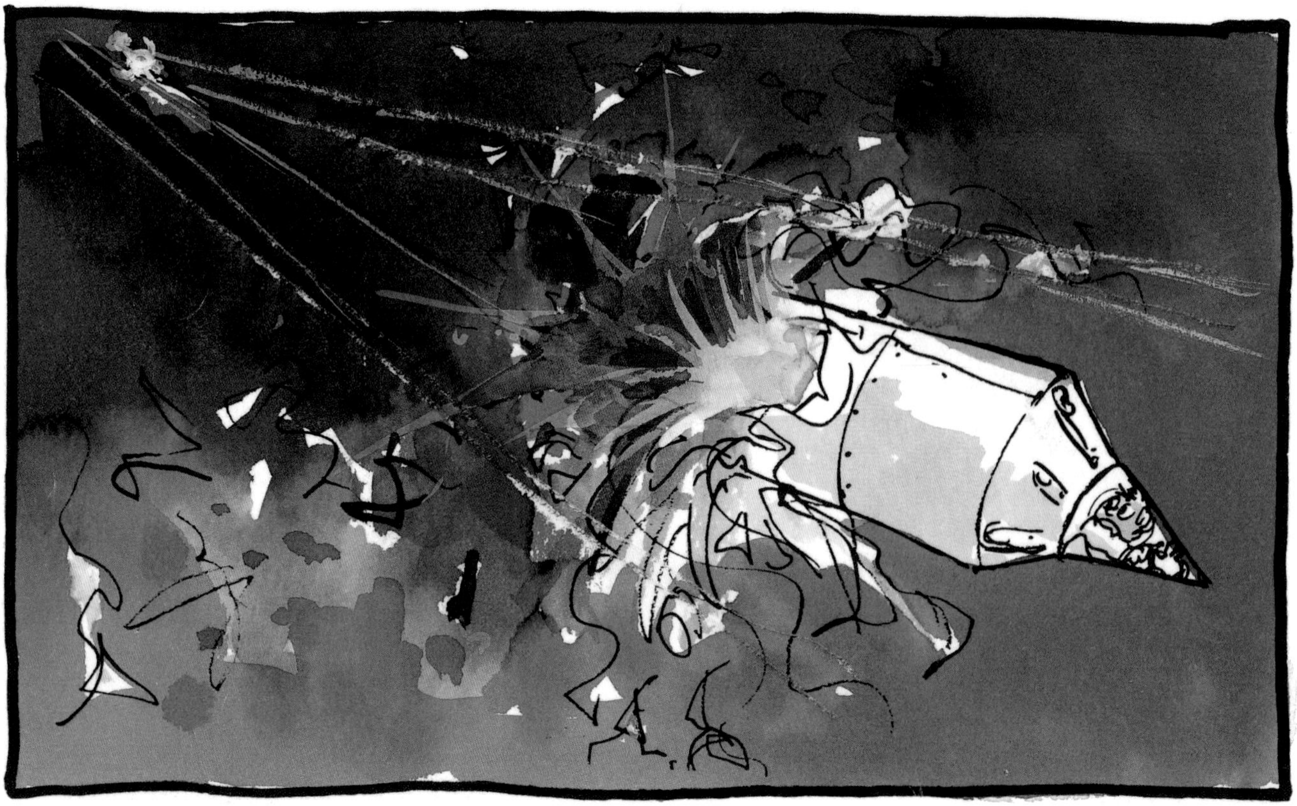

And then his fore.

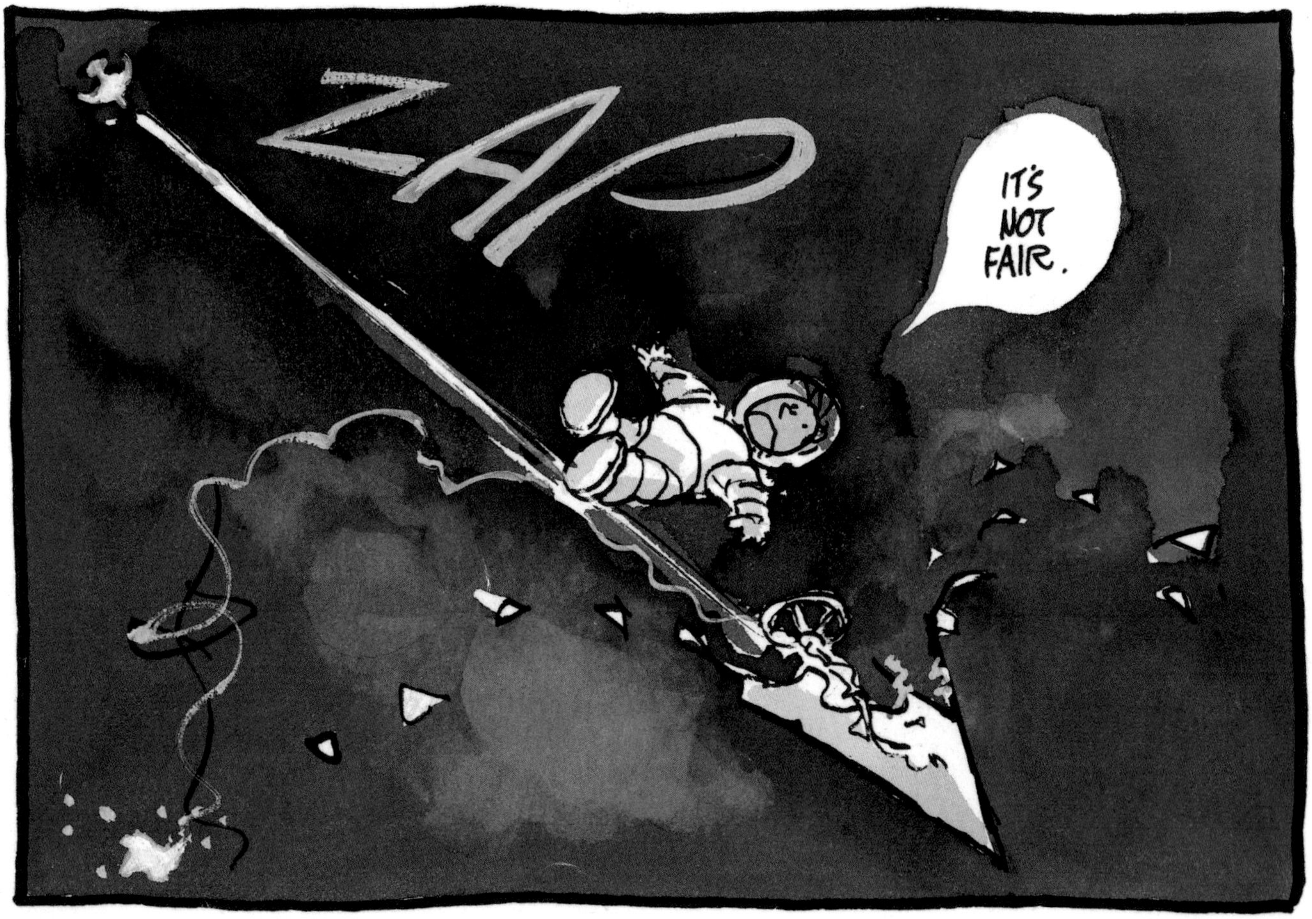
ZAP
IT'S NOT FAIR.

The leftover Martians zoomed in on him. The situation was hopeless.

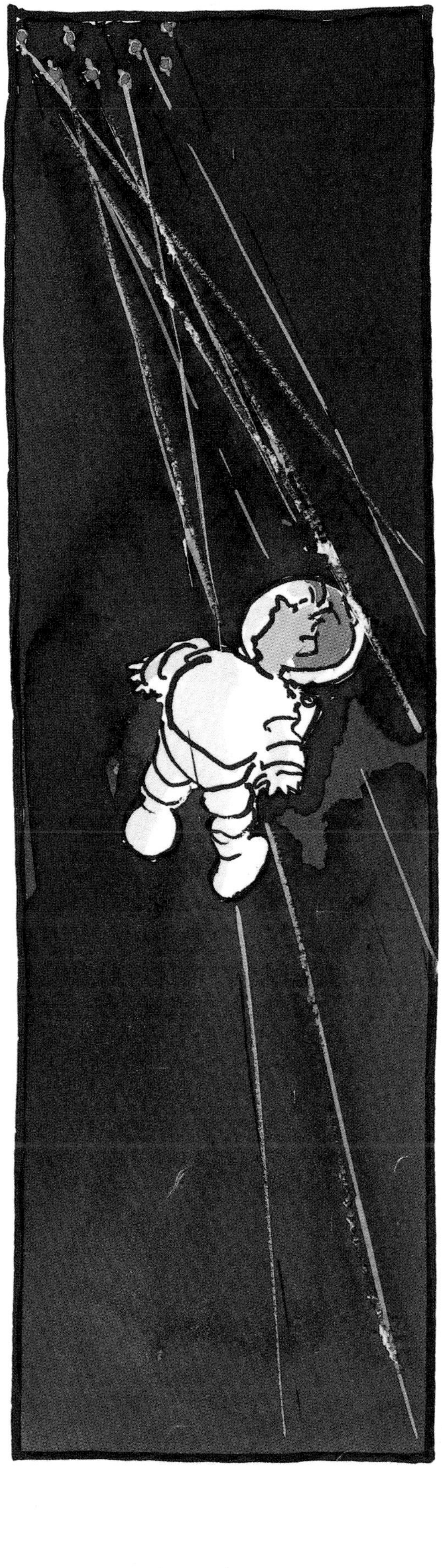

Raymond knew he had one last chance to save himself. He switched on his backpack-autopower-vaporwriter.

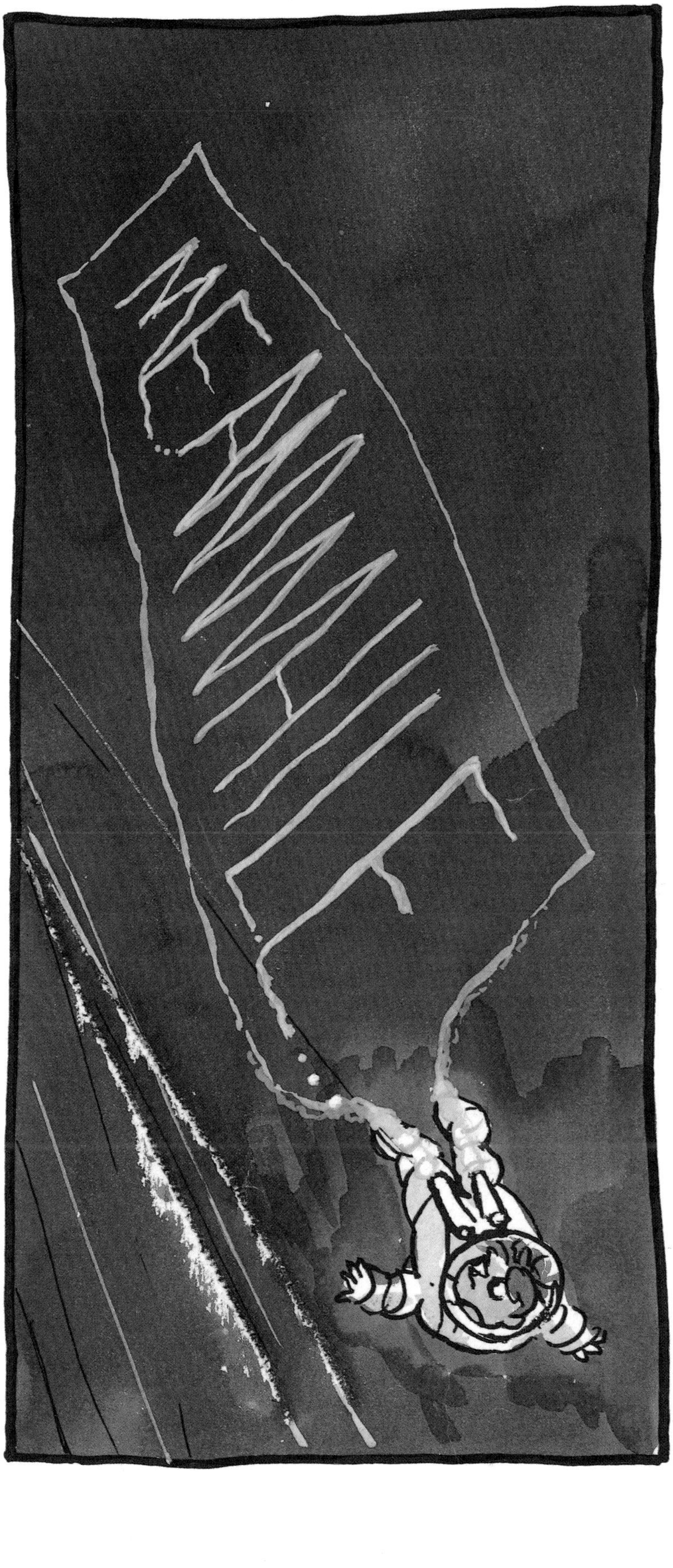
MEANWHILE

Raymond was walking
the plank again.

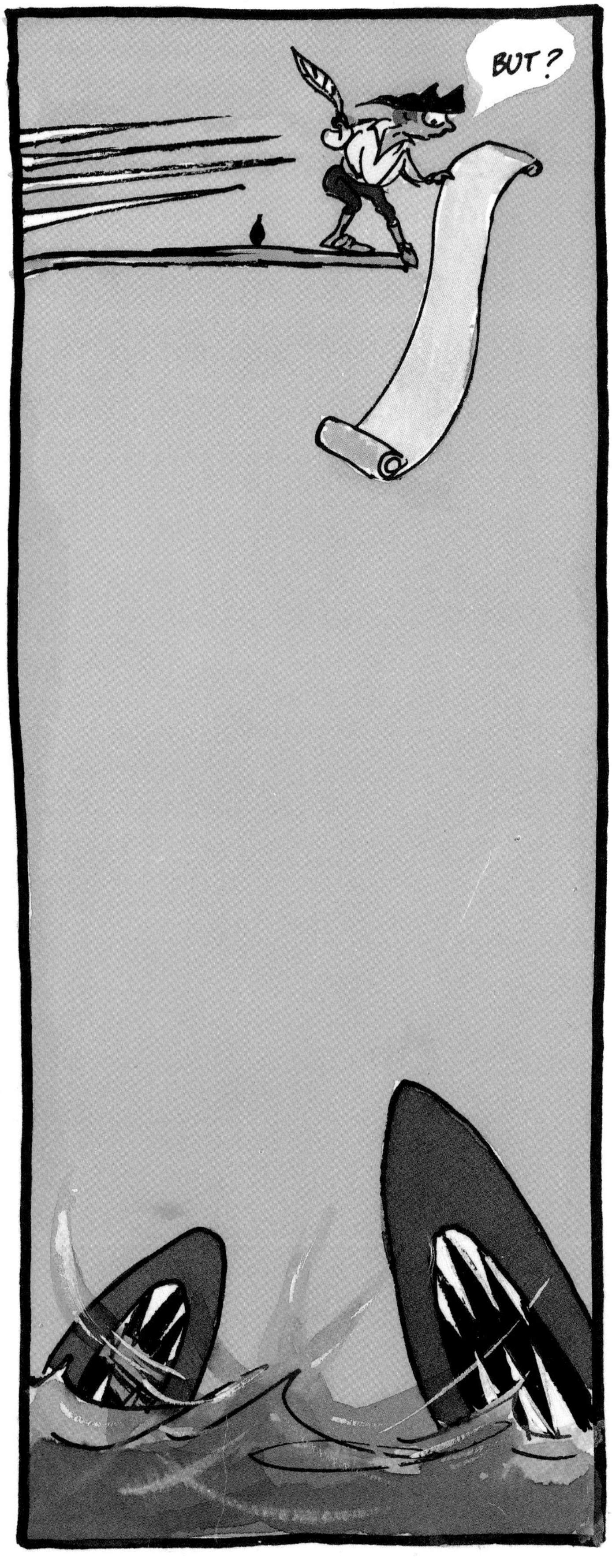
BUT?

Over he went into
the shark-infested sea.
The situation was hopeless.

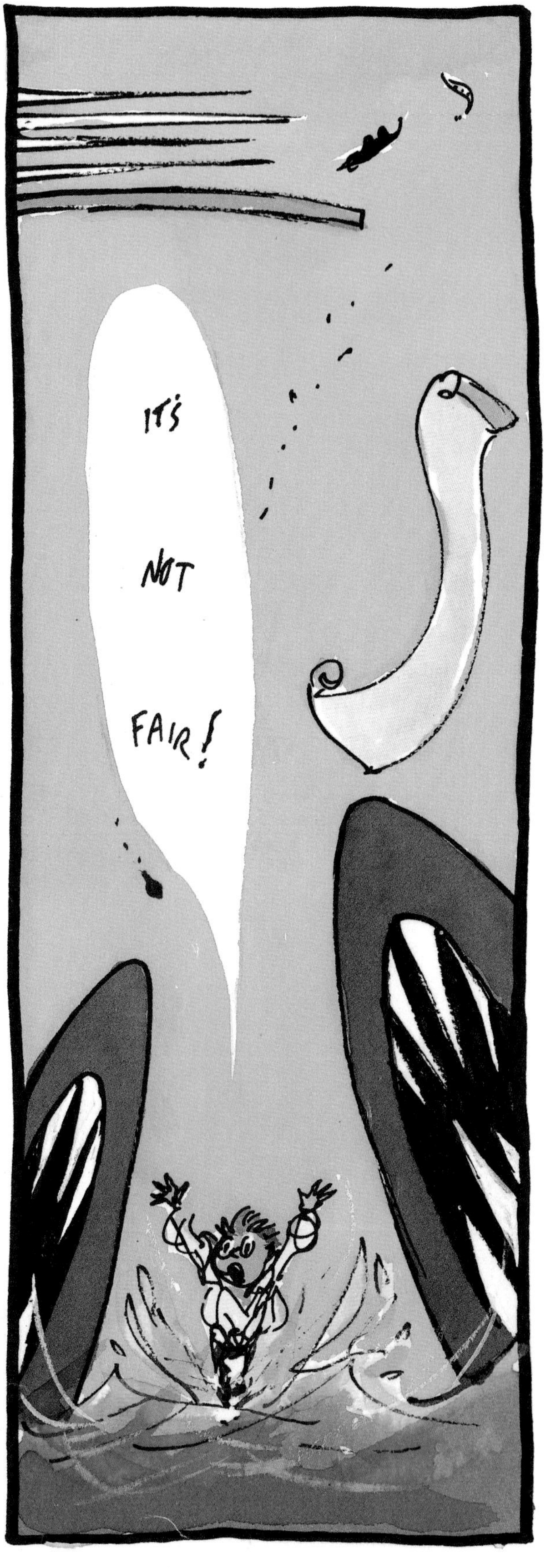
IT'S NOT FAIR!

Raymond knew he had one last chance to save himself. He dipped his finger into the vial of ink and printed on the side of the ship:

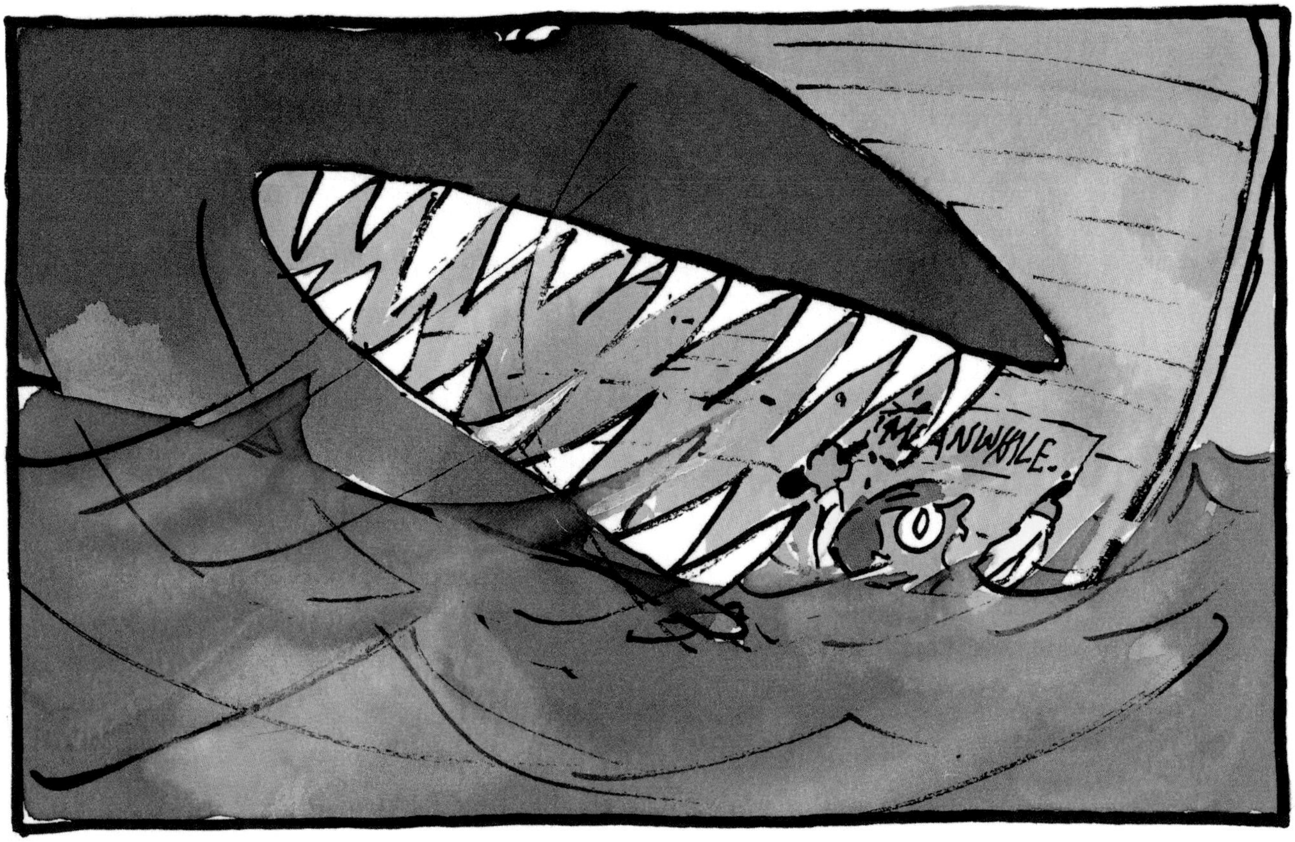
MEANWHILE..

Raymond was out West again.

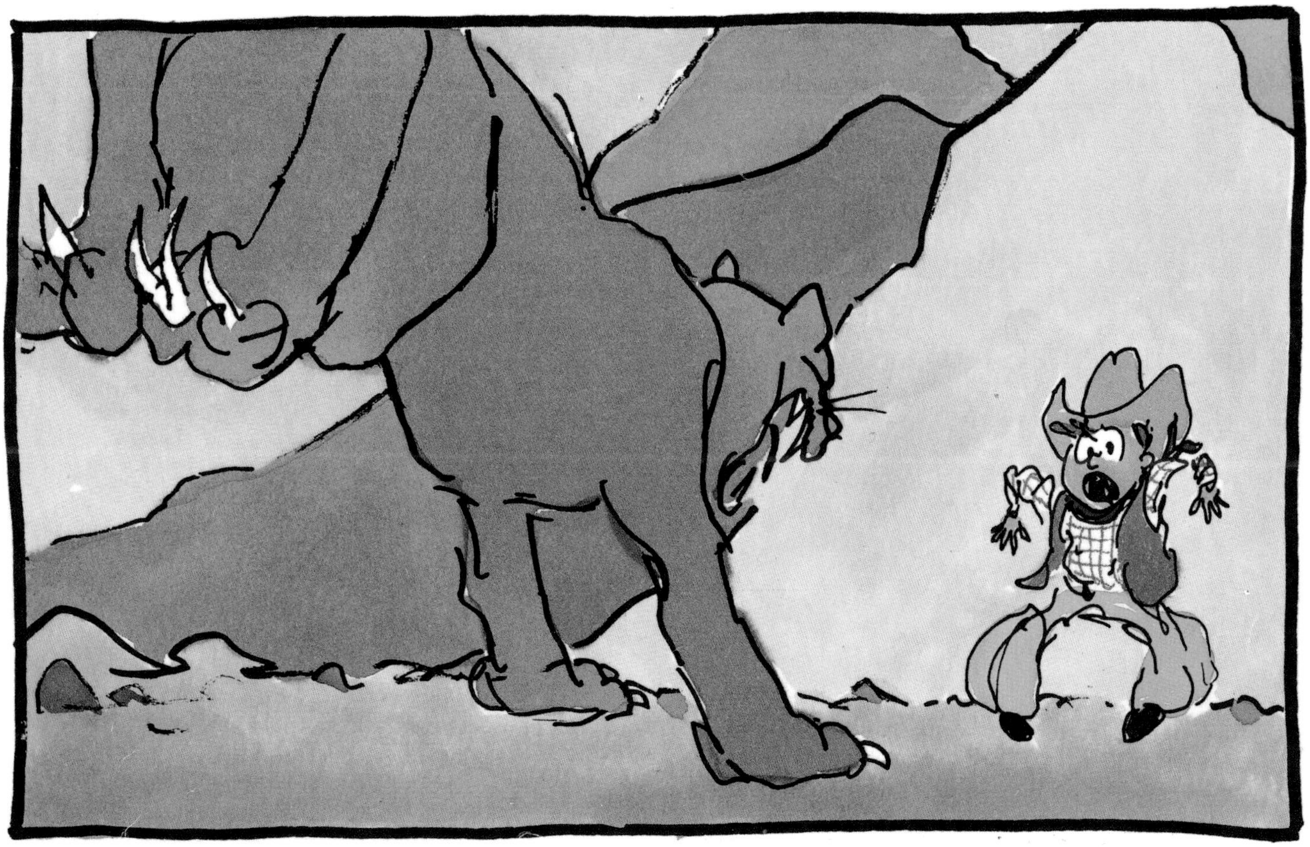

The mountain lion gulped him down in one bite. Raymond was swallowed alive.

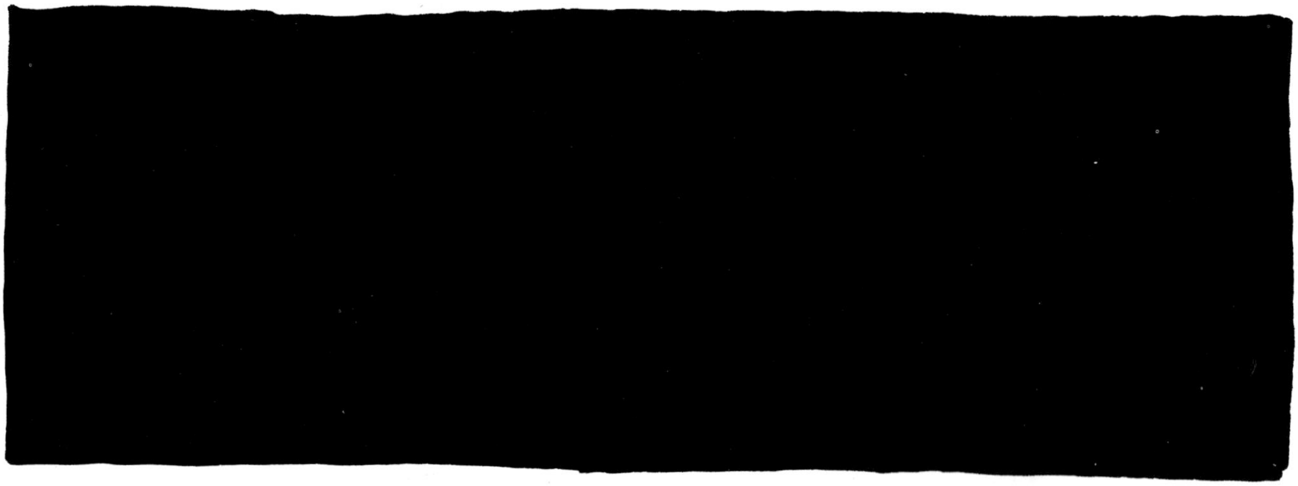

He felt around in his holster for the rusty bullet. It wasn't there. The situation was hopeless.

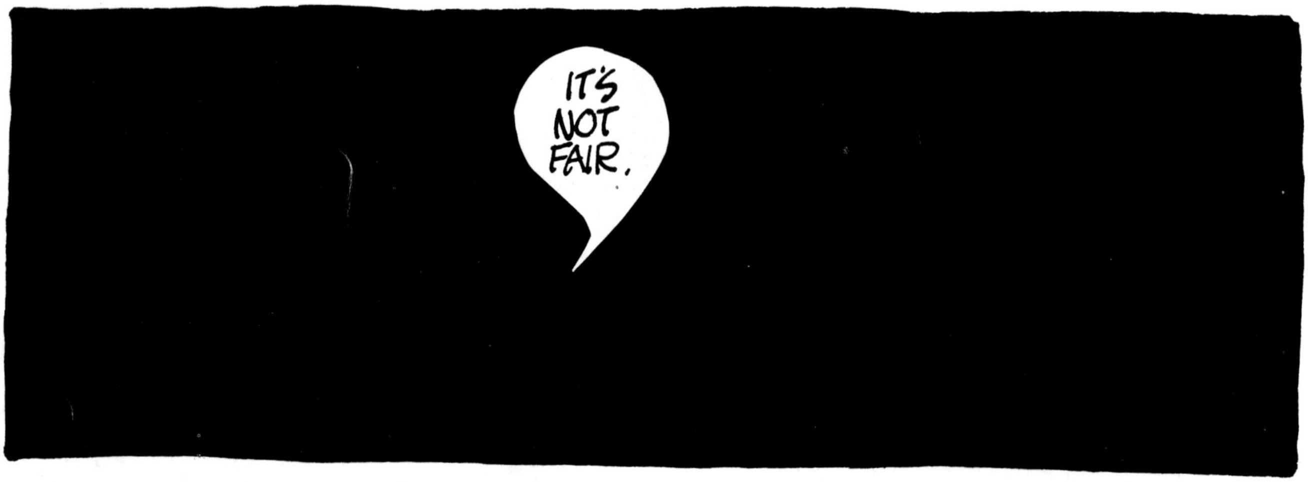
IT'S NOT FAIR.

Raymond knew he had one last chance to save himself. He took off a cowboy boot. With the pointy nail of his big toe, he carved out on the lion's tummy:

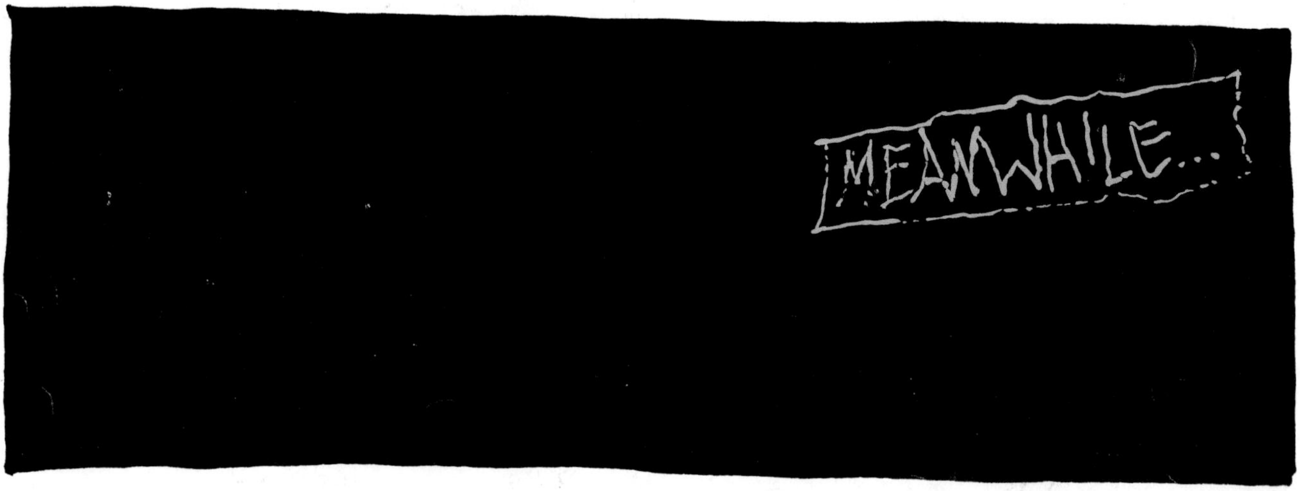
MEANWHILE...

Raymond was ducking missiles in outer space again.

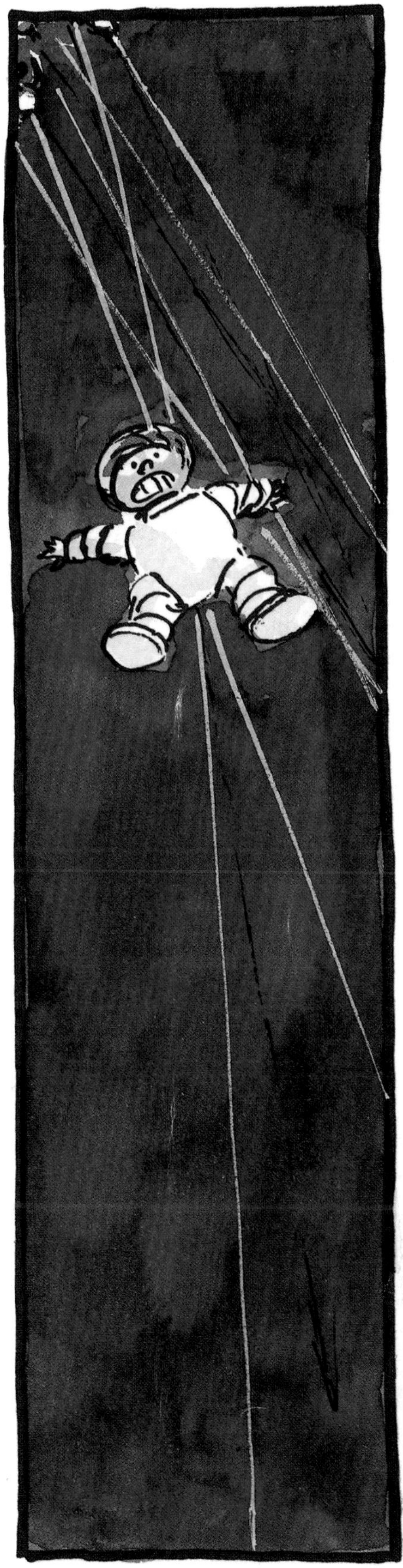

But that wasn't the worst part. The worst part was that his backpack-autopower-vapor-writer had failed.

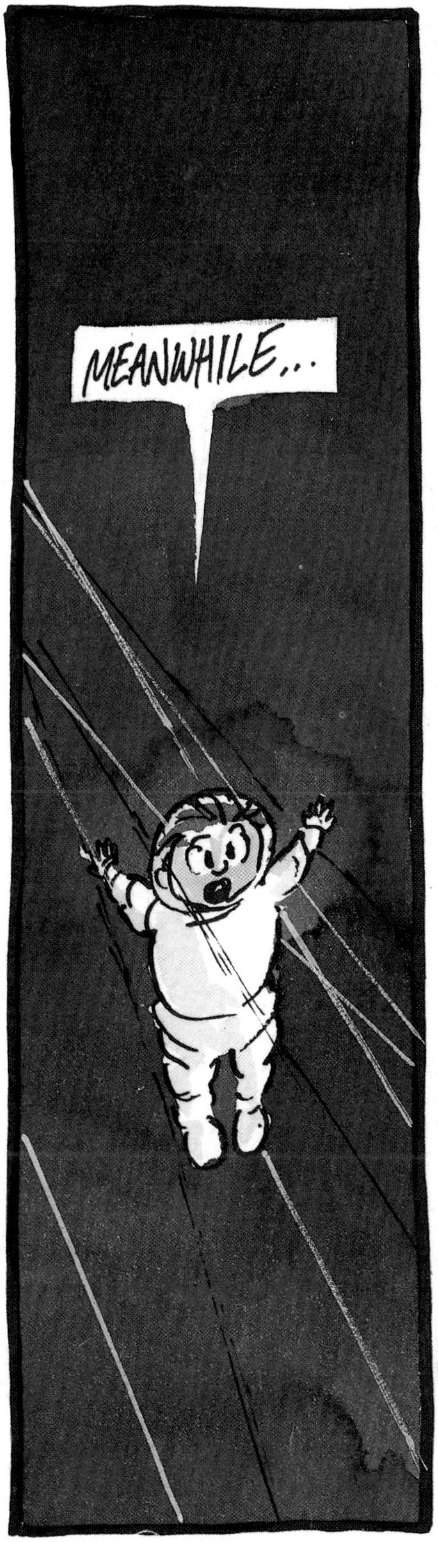
MEANWHILE...

But nothing happened. Raymond had used up his MEANWHILES...

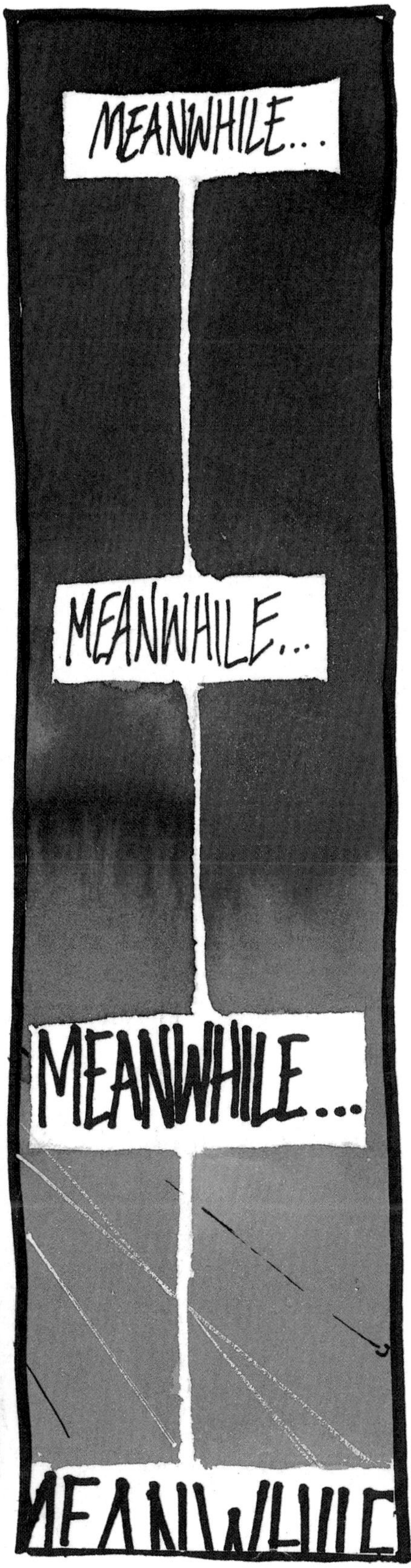
MEANWHILE...
MEANWHILE...
MEANWHILE...

He was falling a thousand feet a second. Right toward his house.

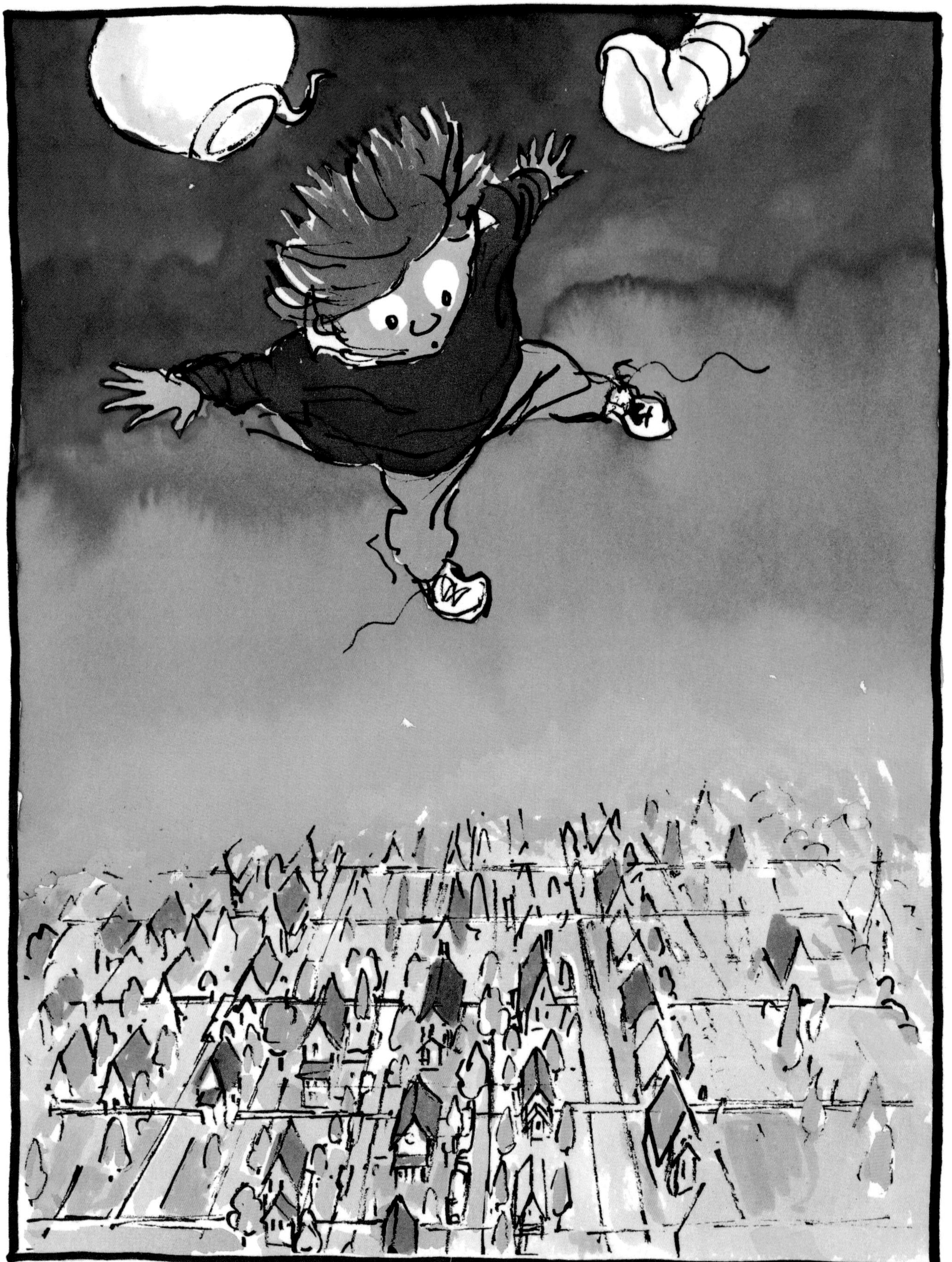

He was going to crash through the roof.

His mother would kill him if he made a mess of the house. The situation was hopeless.

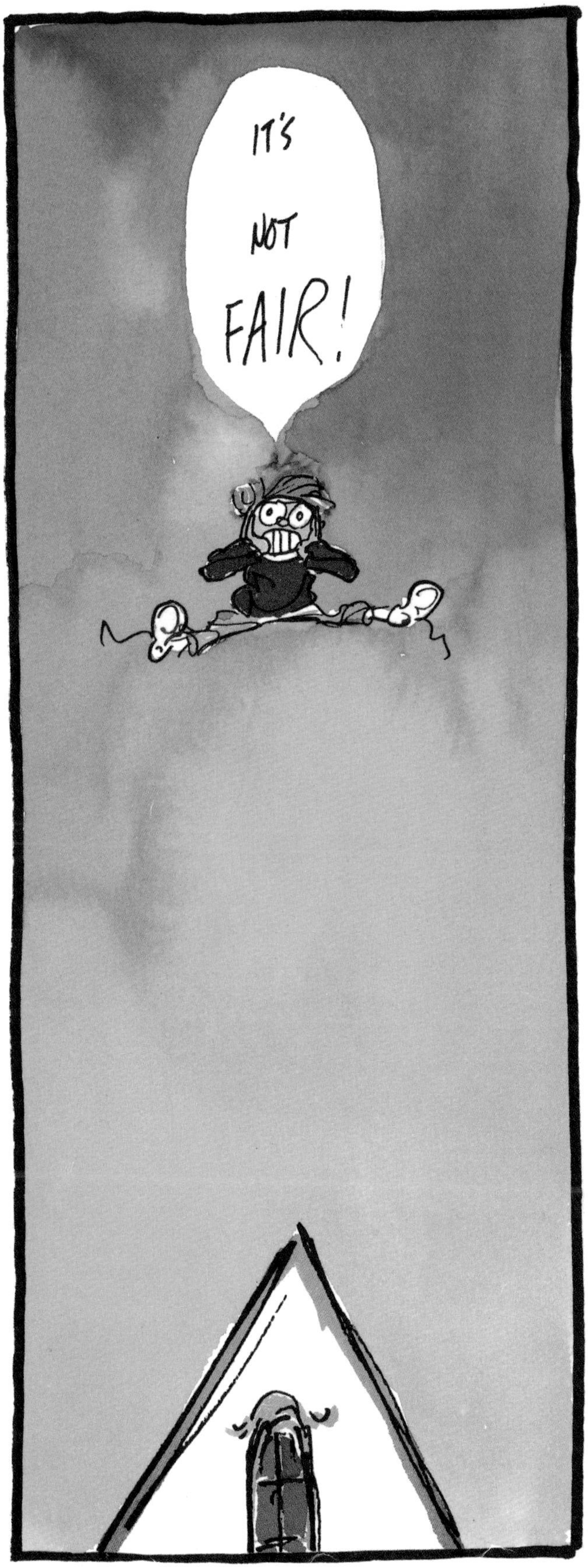
IT'S NOT FAIR!

Raymond knew he had one last chance to save himself. He shouted as loud as he could:

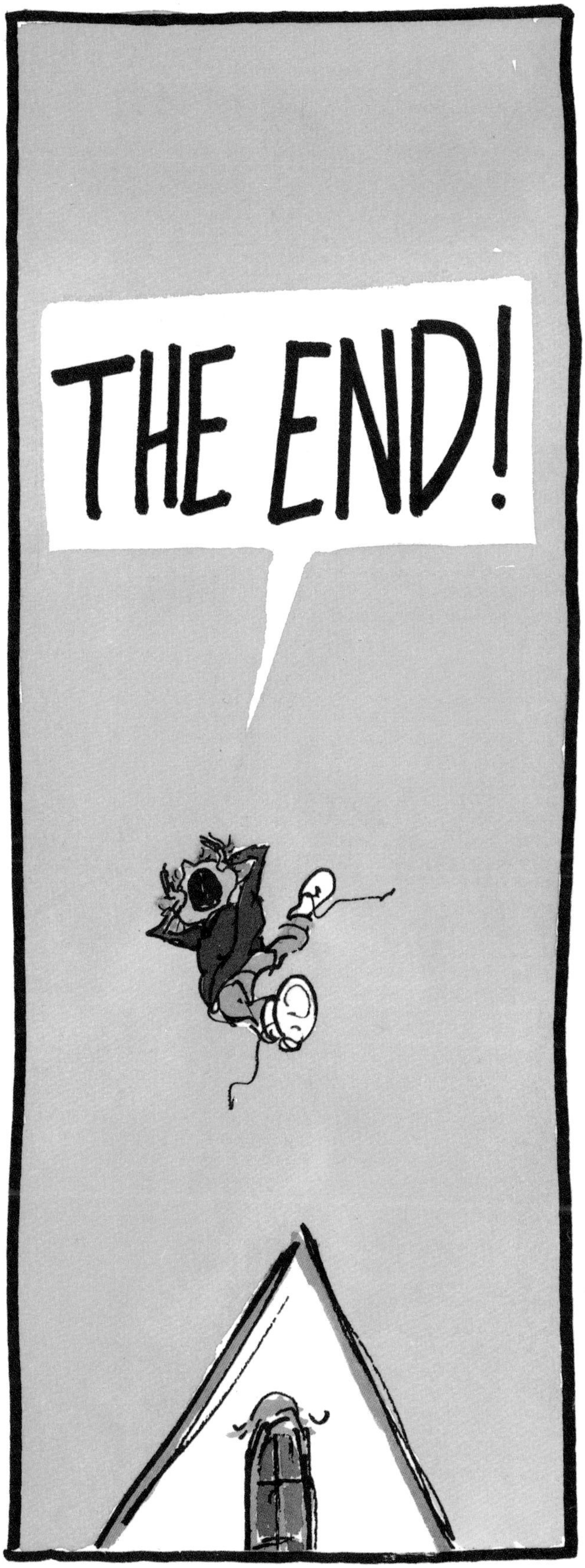
THE END!

It worked. Raymond was back in his room.

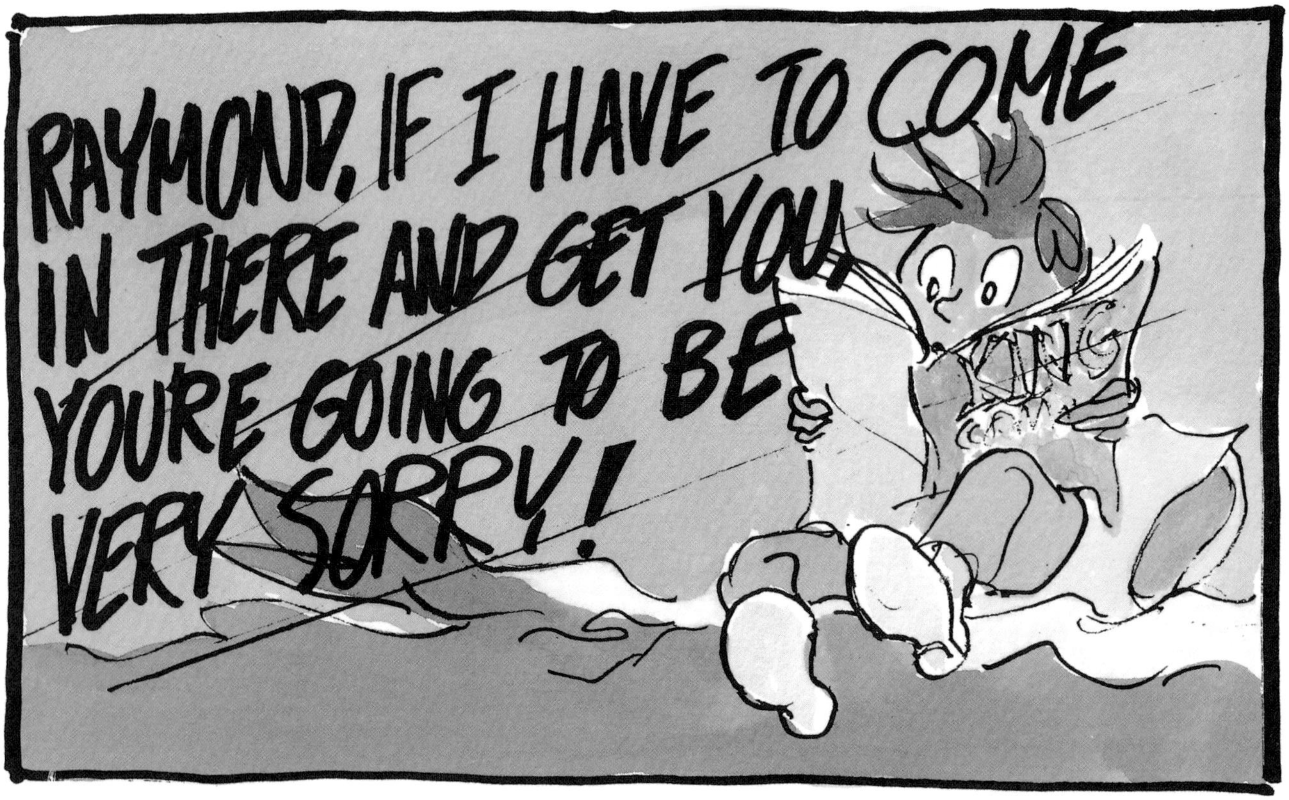
RAYMOND, IF I HAVE TO COME IN THERE AND GET YOU, YOU'RE GOING TO BE VERY SORRY!

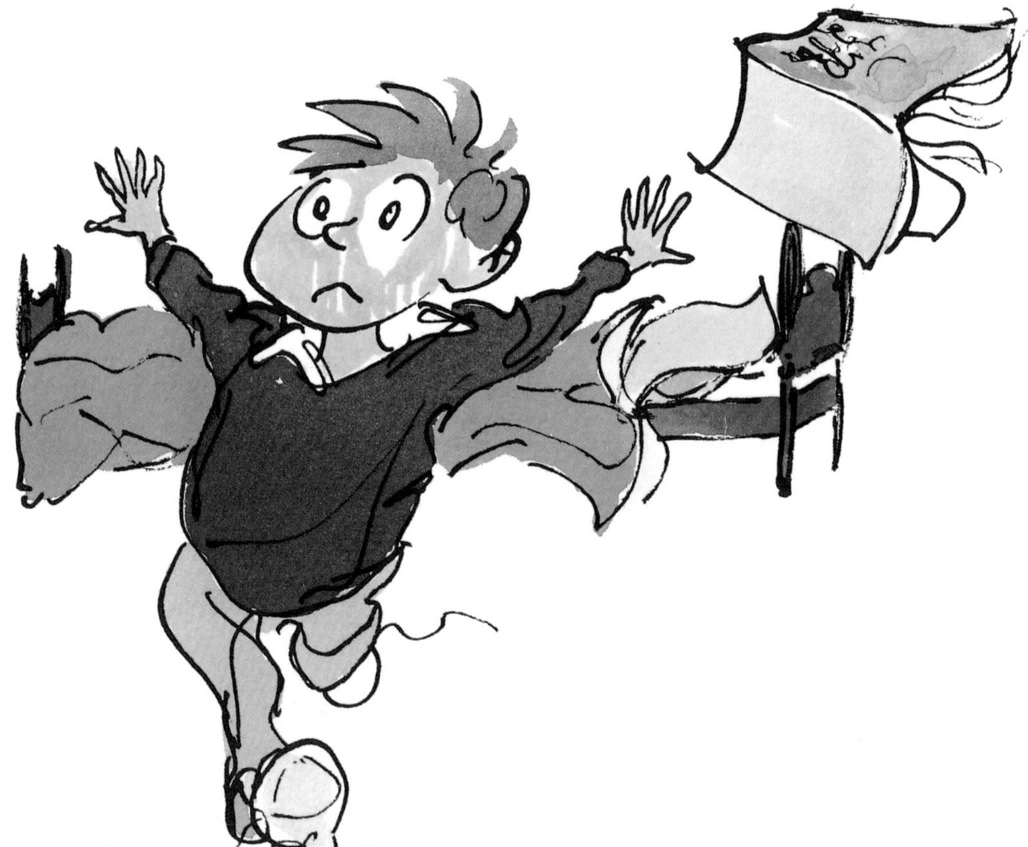

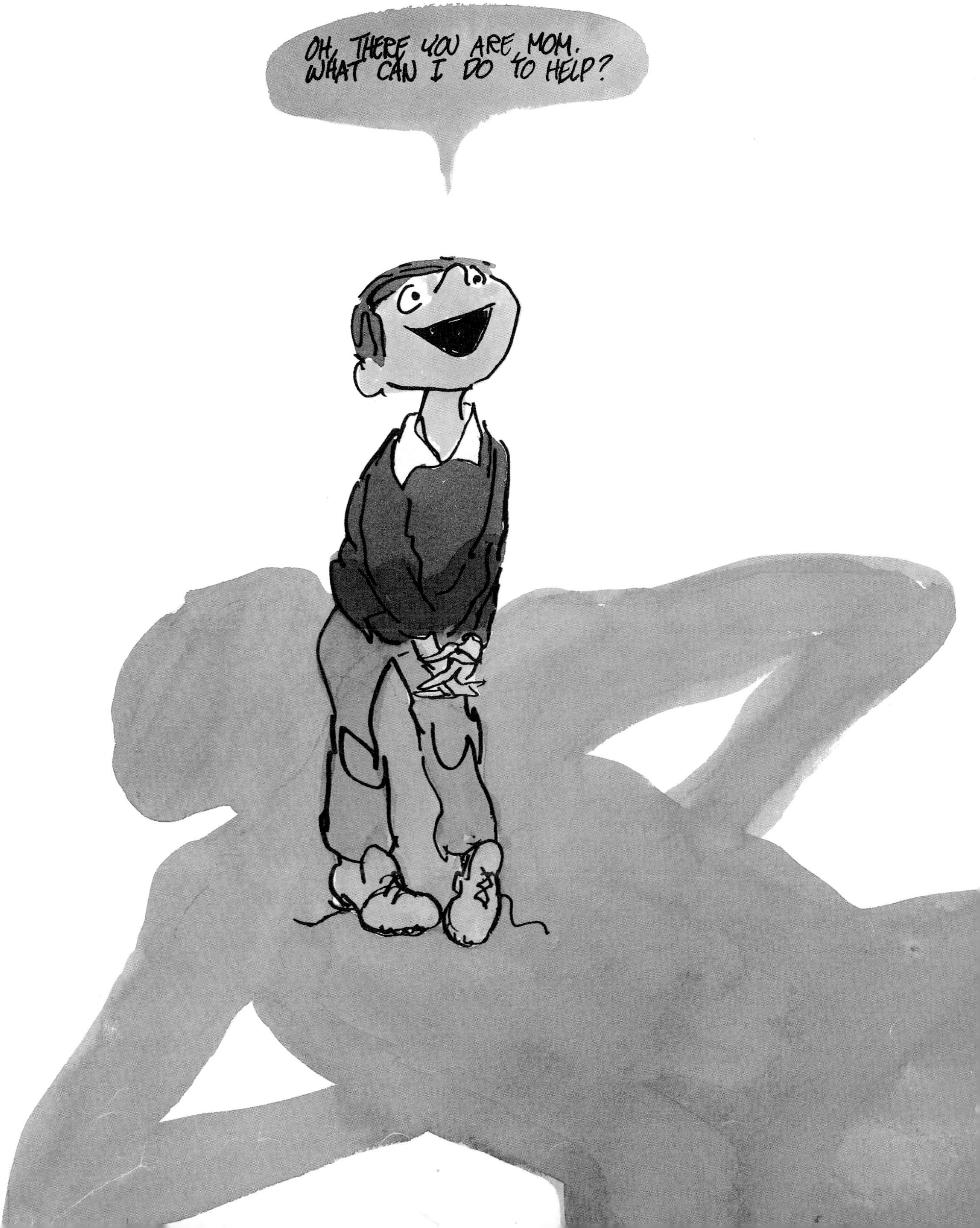
OH, THERE YOU ARE, MOM. WHAT CAN I DO TO HELP?